O.M.G
OH MY GODMOTHER

THE SPELL BIND

Also from the Oh My Godmother series

The Glitter Trap

The Magic Mistake

O·M·G

★ OH MY GODMOTHER ★

★THE★
SPELL
★BIND★

By Barbara Brauner
and James Iver Mattson

Illustrated by
Abigail Halpin

Disney ★ HYPERION ★ Los Angeles ★ New York

First Edition
1 3 5 7 9 10 8 6 4 2
G475-5664-5-14227
Printed in the United States of America

Text is set in Fairfield Light.

Library of Congress Cataloging-in-Publication Data
Brauner, Barbara.
The Spell bind/by Barbara Brauner and James Iver Mattson;
illustrated by Abigail Halpin.—First edition.
pages cm.—(Oh my godmother; [book 3])
Summary: "Lacey Unger-Ware has broken one of the Fairy Godmother rules,
and if she doesn't help fulfill Martin Shembly's wish, there will be a
chilly magical price to pay"—Provided by publisher.
ISBN 978-1-4231-6476-0 (hardback)
[1. Fairy godmothers—Fiction. 2. Magic—Fiction. 3. Wishes—Fiction.
4. Home schooling—Fiction. 5. Humorous stories.] I. Mattson, James Iver.
II. Halpin, Abigail, illustrator. III. Title.
PZ7.B73786Spe 2014
[Fic]—dc23   2014013000

Visit www.DisneyBooks.com

PROLOGUE

Pop quiz: My name is Lacey Unger-Ware, and I am a(n):

a) fairy-godmother-in-training

b) normal sixth grader

c) intern at the Highland Park Zoo

d) assistant at my parents' restaurant, the Hungry Moose

e) babysitter to my cute/annoying five-year-old sister,
Madison

f) all of the above

The answer is: f) all of the above.

It's crazy, right? How can one person do all this stuff? Even *five* people would have trouble doing all this stuff.

You're probably thinking I should be able to wave my magic wand and get everything done. But magic never makes things easier—it makes things harder, and stranger, and more likely to blow up in your face.

So maybe the answer isn't f) at all. Maybe it's h) for help!

CHAPTER 1

For the first time ever, in like hundreds and hundreds of years, the Godmothers' League is letting a student be homeschooled instead of sent away to the Godmother Academy.

That student is me.

And where there's a student, there's got to be a teacher. *My* teacher is Katarina Sycorax, who's three inches tall with beautiful butterfly wings and a bad attitude. (By bad attitude, I mean she's cranky.)

I've had cranky teachers before, and I bet you have, too. But yours probably wasn't living on top of your dresser in your bedroom. And I'm sure yours didn't cut the arm off your favorite teddy bear to make herself a fur coat. Or threaten to turn you into an elephant if you didn't memorize your assignment. (Because everyone knows that elephants have excellent memories.)

For me, it's like the school day is twenty-four hours long and the bell never rings.

Katarina and I have been waiting for weeks to find out who my new fairy godmother client is, and we're both getting pretty antsy about it. When I get antsy, I chew my fingernails. When Katarina gets antsy, she yells. Like, all the time. Right now, she's yelling about my book report, which she's also stomping on.

"This stinks! Did you even bother to read *Godmothering During the Renaissance?*"

"Of course I did!"

The old, dusty book is still on my desk. Katarina flies over and tells it, "Book! Show me how far Lacey read!"

When the pages flip open and stop at Chapter Two, Katarina gives me an accusing look.

"All right! I fell asleep! But it was so boring! Why do I need to know what kind of gloves they wore in the fifteenth century?"

"Because you do, that's why. I want you to rewrite this book report by tomorrow! After you actually read the book!" Katarina shakes her finger at me. "You don't seem to appreciate the sacrifices I'm making for you. I'm sleeping in your jewelry box. I have to hide from your excruciatingly loud family. And your cat has tried to eat me fourteen times!"

Feeling guilty, I pick up the godmothering history book and say, "All right! All right! I *do* appreciate what you're doing for me. I'll finish this. I'm sure *you* read it cover to cover."

"Of course I did. I was an excellent student."

The old book shudders a little, and the pages flip back to Chapter One. I look at Katarina, annoyed. "You stopped at Chapter *One*?"

Katarina slams the book shut and shrugs. "I agree; it's a little dull. But until you get your client, that's all there is."

"When's that going to be? Me getting a client, I mean."

"I keep telling you, it's up to the godmothers. It could be next month, or there could be a messenger at the door right now."

There's a loud knock at my closed bedroom door. I gawk at it in surprise.

Katarina snaps, "Well, answer it!"

I go to the door, a little excited. I hope I get to help somebody nice, somebody who really needs me.

But it's not a messenger standing on the other side of the door; it's my sister, Madison. She's wearing one of her many, many pink tutus and has a feather in her hair. "Ta-da! We're twins!"

"We who?"

Then I hear a small, sad meow.

I glance down and see my unhappy-looking orange cat, Julius, sitting at Madison's feet. He's also wearing a pink tutu, and Madison has Scotch-taped a feather to his head. "Madison! You're humiliating him!"

"He looks beautiful."

"He looks stupid!" I pick him up and hold him in my lap. "You can't play with him like this. He's not your cat."

"But *you* never play with him anymore."

I hate it when my five-year-old sister is right. Julius hasn't been able to come into my room in weeks, because whenever he does, he tries to eat Katarina. (She's the best kitty treat he's ever had.)

I tell Madison, "Well, I'm going to play with him now."

I close the door and sit on my bed with Julius in my arms. He purrs—and then he stiffens and makes a chirping sound. He's spotted Katarina on my dresser; it's all I can do to hold on to him.

Katarina points at the door. "That beast has to go!"

"But I miss him! And it's his room, too."

"Not anymore. Evict him!"

I can't evict Julius; instead, I have a brilliant idea. I pull my magic wand out of my pocket. It's about the size of a pin (usually they shrink the fairy to match the wand, but I've been able to avoid that so far).

"What do you think you're doing?" Katarina asks.

"Fixing our Julius problem." I raise the wand and chant, "This room is more bearable, when Katarina tastes terrible." But I don't toss the spell at Julius—I toss it at Katarina.

Katarina's eyes cross when the spell hits her, and then they uncross and glare at me. "Lacey, you've entirely violated the student-teacher relationship. You are dis—"

Before I can stop him, Julius leaps away from me and half swallows Katarina, whose little feet kick wildly. Since her head is in Julius's throat, I can't hear the rest of what she's hollering. Was she about to say: *You are disgusting, disobedient, disappointing,* or some other *dis* word entirely?

A second later Julius spits Katarina out. She lands on the dresser, her glasses askew and her hair dripping with cat spit. Shaking his head like he's just tasted a rotten lemon, Julius gives Katarina one more sniff, and then, revolted, he jumps off the dresser onto the bed next to me.

Katarina straightens her glasses and finally finishes the sentence she started: "You are disgraceful!"

Disgraceful! A *dis* word I didn't even think of. "Maybe I'm disgraceful, but my spell worked!"

Julius curls up on the bed and goes to sleep. He's obviously decided that rotten-lemon-flavored fairies aren't worth the trouble.

Katarina pulls a little brush out of my jewelry box and yanks it through her hair to get out the drool. "Fine! The fleabag can stay! Have fun setting your alarm clock for 12:01."

"For 12:01?"

"You should know by now that every fairy godmother spell ends at midnight. And I refuse to be eaten by a cat while I'm sleeping—it's so discombobulating!" (Another *dis* word!) "So you'll have to recast your spell at 12:01."

"Every day?"

"Consider it homework."

Katarina crawls into the little jewelry box she uses as a bed. She mutters to herself, "I don't taste terrible! Fairies taste delicious." Then she licks her arm and shudders. "Ew. I *do* taste terrible!" The jewelry box snaps closed.

I sigh and set my alarm clock for 12:01. Now I even have homework in the middle of the night.

CHAPTER 2

I rush into homeroom just as the first bell rings. Katarina used to come to school in my pocket, but she stopped doing that weeks ago. She told me, "As long as you don't have a client, I might as well stay home and enjoy my miserable new life." (Katarina's exact words.)

My best friend, Sunny Varden, leans over as I slide into my chair. "Why are you late?"

"I'm not late!" I snap.

"Okay, you're not late. Why are you crabby?" Sunny knows me better than anybody.

"Sorry. I had to get up at midnight to do a magic spell, and then I couldn't go back to sleep."

"Fun magic or homeschool magic?"

"Homeschool magic."

Sunny gives me a sympathetic smile. "Katarina's *tough.*"

There are only a few people who know about me and Katarina, and Sunny is one of them. Another is Paige Harrington, who was my first fairy godmother client and is now my other best friend.

Oh, there *is* one more person who knows about me and Katarina: the school's former principal. But after I helped Principal Nazarino have her dream wedding with the basketball coach, they went to Hawaii for their honeymoon and decided to stay there forever. So now we have Principal Conehurst . . . whose voice suddenly blares out of the TV screen at the front of the classroom, which is showing a picture of the flag on the school's front lawn.

"Good morning, Lincoln Middle School! Please rise for the Pledge of Allegiance."

We used to do the pledge with no help from the television. But Principal Conehurst likes the morning webcast. It's sort of a fake news program, just for the school. If Principal Conehurst was the only one doing the webcast, it wouldn't be so bad. He's got a low, rumbly voice that's easy to ignore.

But after the pledge, the screen cuts to the school "newsroom," which is actually a table in the library. Makayla Brandice, my least-favorite cheerleader, sits at a microphone pretending to be a newscaster and loving every second of it. "Good morning, Lincoln! This is Makayla Brandice, your eyes and ears on the school." Now *there's* a voice that's not easy to ignore. She's done so many cheers that her volume is set at extra loud and

extra-extra irritating. "Today's lunch menu is pasta with meat sauce and cheesy breadsticks. The side dishes are green beans and applesauce. Give me a Y-U-M for YUM!"

I put my head on my desk and moan. "Wake me when sixth grade is over."

Sunny pats my arm and says, "Let's go to the mall after school. That'll make you feel better."

"I can't. Katarina says I can only miss magic homeschooling if I have something for real school."

Sunny frowns. "Magic is cool—but that means you're going to school twice every day. Once is hard enough."

"I agree a million percent."

On the screen, Makayla shuffles through her papers. "And don't forget to be a Lincolnite!"

"What's a Lincolnite?" I ask Sunny.

"It's Principal Conehurst's new name for all the after-school clubs."

"Can't we just call them *after-school clubs*?"

Sunny shrugs. "*Lincolnite* is fancier."

Makayla talks a little louder on the TV, almost as if she can hear us interrupting her. "This afternoon is Lincolnite sign-up day in the school parking lot! There's a club for everyone, even if you're a total loser!" She smiles at the camera like she's just said something really sweet and thoughtful.

Sunny turns to me and says, "Lacey! You should sign up for some clubs!"

"I don't have time to join a club. I barely have time to eat."

"Think about it. Katarina says you can skip magic home-schooling if you have something for school—and the clubs are a part of school."

I *do* think about it. On the one hand, joining a bunch of clubs would give me more work to do. On the other hand, every time I'm at a club meeting, I won't be with Katarina.

It's a no-brainer! "Sunny, you're a genius! I'll text Paige, too."

After our last classes, Sunny, Paige, and I meet at the edge of the school parking lot. Paige's blond hair shines in the sun—she's the prettiest girl I know. And even though she's head cheerleader, she's also really nice. At our school, at least, nice and cheerleader don't usually go together. (See: Makayla.)

A long, long row of folding tables has been set up in the middle of the parking lot, with a huge sign in front: WELCOME LINCOLNITES!

There are tables for the French Club, the Spanish Club, the Practical Jokers Society, the Science Club, Craft-N-Crunch, the Anime-Maniacs, the Weightlifting Club, Speedcubing, the Toast Club (which isn't about making speeches; it's really about making the jam-and-butter kind), the Drama Club, the Uni-Cyclones, the History Club, Origami for World Peace, and Soccer Boot Camp. There's even a table for the school webcast, where admiring kids cluster around Makayla like she's a celebrity. Makayla was popular before the morning show—now she's a TV star, or at least a webcast star.

"How many clubs do you want to join?" Paige asks me.

"One for every day of the week."

Paige looks surprised. "Seriously?"

"Any club would be better than being home with Katarina."

"I hear Makayla needs an assistant for the webcast," Paige says, trying not to smile.

"Correction: *almost* any club would be better than Katarina."

As we all walk along the tables, we decide to join a club together. Unlike me, Sunny and Paige only want to join one.

(*They're* not trying to get out of fairy godmother homeschooling.) We eventually decide to sign up for Craft-N-Crunch, which is run by Mrs. Fleecy, the school secretary. Mrs. Fleecy's plan is for us to make jewelry (the craft part) and eat Rice Krispies treats (the crunch part). We like this plan.

"One club down, four to go!" I say.

Then we stop in front of the table for the Boy with the Longest Eyelashes in the World Club. (Joking!) It's actually the table where Scott Dearden, the cutest boy in school, is signing up people for the Uni-Cyclones while riding a unicycle backward. He's *that* talented.

"Hi, Lacey!" Scott calls out to me. "You're signing up, right? We'll have fun!"

Sunny smiles, Paige nudges me, and I turn bright red. I have to say right here: Scott is not my boyfriend. We're just friends.

"Gee, Scott, I don't think I'm coordinated enough for a unicycle."

"If you can ride a bike, you can ride one of these! I'm a good teacher."

"But I don't *have* a unicycle."

"You can buy one really cheap online."

I hesitate and then sign his list. Maybe I'll get killed, but unicycles do look like fun. Plus I'll get to spend time with Scott. Don't tell Sunny and Paige I said that.

A couple of minutes later, I also sign up for the French Club (*ooh la la!*) and the Donate a Sheep Club (*ewe la la!*), and I just need one more to fill out my schedule.

We walk up to a table that has an enormous sign made out of aluminum foil: FUTURE FLYERS. The kid at the table, Martin Shembly, sees us and waves excitedly. "Hi, guys! You're just in time for the demonstration!"

Paige, Sunny, and I haven't known Martin very long. What I mainly know is that he's really brainy. He plays the violin and is both a Trekkie and a Lord of the Rings fanatic. He's also funny and, beneath his thick glasses, sort of cute.

Martin and Sunny have been hanging out some while I've been busy with homeschooling. They watch the super duper extended versions of the Lord of the Rings movies at Sunny's house, and I know she kind of likes him. But that's all I know, because I've been a horrible friend lately.

Usually, when you're best friends with someone, you know every detail about what's going on with them. But *usually* you don't have a three-inch-tall fairy living in your bedroom and taking up all your time.

We walk closer to Martin's table and see that he's holding a G.I. Joe doll (correction: *action figure*—boys get upset when you call them dolls) that has a little backpack strapped to its back. Maybe it's a parachute.

Sunny asks Martin, "Didn't your mom say you don't have time for a club?"

"What she doesn't know won't hurt her. This is going to be *maar*! That's Elvish for great and excellent!"

Just when I thought Martin couldn't get any more unusual, he starts talking Elf! No wonder people think he's a little strange.

"What's the club about?" Paige asks.

"We're going to build a real, working, low-cost jetpack! I've got the plans all drawn up—I just need six club members with leaf blowers," Martin explains. "And by the end of the month, we'll be flying!"

Sunny picks up the clipboard with the sign-up sheet. "How many people do you have so far?"

"Well, *no one*. That's why I'm doing this demonstration." Martin picks up a bullhorn and turns it on, sending out an ear-shattering screech of feedback. Kids all around us look at him and cover their ears. "Everybody! Prepare to be amazed!"

He holds the G.I. Joe figure in the air. "By the end of the month, my goal is to make a working, full-size version of *this*!" The kids watch, curious, as he pushes a button on G.I. Joe's backpack.

But Joe doesn't fly—he just makes a really, really, *really* loud farting noise: *POOOT!*

Every kid in the parking lot laughs. I do, too. I can't help myself—farts are funny. But when Martin turns bright red and looks miserable, I feel guilty.

When the laughter finally dies down (it takes a long time),

Sunny tells Martin, "It almost worked. And nobody thought *you* made the sound."

At the edge of the parking lot, Makayla peers into her cell phone camera and says, loudly, "This is Makayla Brandice, your eyes and ears of the school. And *that* was a demonstration of a so-called jetpack."

The phone of almost every kid in the parking lot—including mine—buzzes with a school webcast alert. I look at it and see that Makayla has uploaded a video with the heading "Fartin' Martin." It already has over two hundred clicks, and the numbers are going up every second.

Martin looks away from his own phone, straightens his shoulders, and says, "Onward! Every great invention has a few bumps along the way." He turns to me, Sunny, and Paige hopefully. "You guys are signing up, right? The club meets Thursdays."

Sunny, Paige, and I all look at each other. We like Martin, but that's when Craft-N-Crunch meets. Future flying just can't compete with jewelry and Rice Krispies.

"We can't," I say. "We already signed up with Mrs. Fleecy."

Sunny tells him, "But don't worry! A lot of kids are going to think your club is really great. You won't even miss us."

Then there's another fart from G.I. Joe.

CHAPTER 3

Madison sticks Mom's cell phone into my face: *"POOOT!"* She giggles hysterically.

Mom and Dad stand at the Hungry Moose's prep table, scooping the middles out of dozens of little, round loaves. "Madison! Cut the farts!" Mom yells.

Dad laughs, but he stops when Mom gives him a look. "Madison. Turn off the phone."

"But it's sooooooo funny!"

I peer down at the screen and see that the Fartin' Martin video now has over four thousand views. He's never going to live this down.

Trying to change the subject, I ask Mom and Dad about the scooped-out loaves.

"They're bread bowls for the chili," Dad says.

"And you know what chili makes you do!" Madison squeals as she hits play on the video. The sound of farting fills the kitchen.

"Madison, I mean it!" Mom says. "No more farting!"

Dad and I can't help it: we laugh.

After a moment, Mom laughs, too. "It might not have been the best day to serve beans."

When I get home, I'm greeted by a big KEEP OUT sign on my closed bedroom door. It's in my handwriting, which is odd because I didn't write it. And the door is locked, which is also odd because my door *doesn't* lock.

I knock. "Katarina? Let me in!"

"What's the magic word?" Katarina trills from inside.

I can't believe I have to ask permission to get into my own room. "*Please* let me in."

There's a faint click and the door swings open. I go into my room, not knowing what to expect. I certainly don't expect this. . . .

My small, cozy room—the one where everything is arranged just the way I like it—has been transformed into a gigantic palace bedroom. The walls are covered with tapestries and gold paint. (Knowing Katarina, it's probably real gold.) Glittering crystal chandeliers, lit by flickering candles, hang from the ceiling. And the bed is bigger than any bed I've ever seen.

Katarina, looking tiny, lounges on a silk pillow, reading an equally tiny copy of French *Vogue*. "Hello, Lacey. I've done a little redecorating. Isn't it lovely?"

"Lovely? Where's my stuff? Where's my computer? Where are my clothes?"

"Stop whining. They'll be back at midnight. This is the first time I've had a permanent home, and I want to be comfortable."

"My room *was* comfortable!"

Katarina rolls her eyes.

I think about what she just said. "Wait a minute. What do you mean, it's the first time you've had a permanent home? Don't you have a little house or an apartment someplace? Or a fairy condo?"

Katarina shakes her head. "I'm always on assignment. If I do get a few days off, I stay at the Ritz in Paris."

"You rent a room?"

"No, I stay in a flower arrangement in the Coco Chanel Suite. It's heavenly! I used to stay in an orchid plant in the Elton John Suite, but there were too many parties."

I've never thought about what Katarina's life is like when she's not with me. "So you've never had a home? Or a family?"

"Homes! Families! Stop asking me so many questions!" She waves her hand at my redecorated room. "You're a fairy god-mother now. *This* is a room suitable for a fairy godmother."

I try to look on the bright side. "At least you made me a nice bed," I say.

"Oh, this isn't your bed. This is my bed." Katarina points to a hard little cot in the corner of the room. "That's your bed."

I'm mad again. "I'm not sleeping there, not even just till midnight! It's not fair!"

Katarina smirks. "You mean it's like sleeping in a little, uncomfortable jewelry box?"

Oh. I sort of get that—but why does she need to be so rude? I close my eyes and count to ten, the way Mom does. Actually, I'm so mad that I count to fifteen. Finally I tell Katarina, "I'll work on getting you a better bed. One that doesn't disappear at midnight."

Katarina keeps on smirking. "This bed is just fine. Yes, it will disappear at midnight, but you can magic me up another one when you get up at 12:01 to do your anti-cat spell."

"That's all I need. *More* homework."

"Speaking of homework . . . where is your book report on Renaissance godmothering?"

"Uh."

"Just as I suspected! You're shirking!"

"I am not! I'm just late with my homework!"

"That's shirking!" Katarina flicks her wand, and a thick notebook plops into one of my hands and a pencil into the other. "I

want you to write 'Only jerks shirk their homework' a hundred times."

"Teachers don't say 'jerk'!"

"I do!"

And then—because I'm tired, and still upset about my room—I say something I probably shouldn't. "*Good* teachers don't say 'jerk.'"

Katarina scowls. "I'll show you a good teacher! Write 'Only jerks shirk their homework' a *thousand* times."

I consider writing just the words *Only jerks shirk their homework a thousand times* and handing the notebook back to her, but Katarina looks angry enough that I decide I'd better not risk it. What if she makes me write it ten thousand times? My hand would fall off.

Since my desk is gone, I sit on my hard little cot and start to write. I feel more like Cinderella than a fairy godmother.

CHAPTER 4

At midnight, I don't need my alarm to wake up, because, *THUD!* I fall from where the hard little cot used to be onto the floor. Still groggy, I see that Katarina's gigantic palace bedroom has disappeared, and she's sleeping in the middle of my bed, looking very comfortable.

All I want to do is go back to sleep, but I stumble over and pull my wand out of my backpack. I raise it—ow! My hand hurts from the blister I got writing *only jerks* so many times. Then I chant, "This room is more terrible, when Katarina tastes bearable."

I toss the spell at Katarina, and pink sparkles land all over her. A moment later, she sits up and *growls*.

I know what you're thinking: I messed up. But *you're* completely awake (you are, right?), and I am half asleep. Plus I just whacked my head on the floor. And my hand hurts. You can't blame me for getting my words mixed up a little.

Eek! Katarina's hairy. She's got claws. Her teeth are long and sharp. She's a *bear*. A three-inch-tall bear who wears a dress and has beautiful butterfly wings.

Actually, she's one of the cutest things I've ever seen. She's a beary godmother! I *awww* at her—which makes her growl louder. I stroke her little furry head with my finger. "I know you can't talk, but it's going to be all right."

"I can talk just fine!" my beary godmother shouts. "I've said it before and I'll say it again! You are a disgraceful student!" She looks at her little black claws and yells, "And I just did my nails! Now look at them!"

"I'm sorry! I mixed up the words! It'll wear off at midnight!"

"That's a whole day!" She totters up on her little bear feet and tries to swat at me.

"I'm *sorry*. I'll stay home from school and take care of you."

"I can take care of myself! I might be a bear, but I still have my magic wand." She straightens her glasses, which don't fit very well on her bear nose. She glares at me though them. "Now stop apologizing and make me some porridge."

"Can't you just make it yourself with your magic wand?"

"MAKE ME SOME PORRIDGE!" she snarls, so fiercely

that I back away. Wow, I thought Katarina was cranky before. But Katarina-bear is *super* cranky.

"We don't have any porridge. I can make you oatmeal."

"Oatmeal is porridge, you nitwit," she snaps. "Make me some, now!"

I guess she's as hungry as a bear.

And *that's* why Dad finds me in the kitchen making oatmeal in the middle of the night.

"What are you doing?" he asks, rubbing his sleepy eyes.

"Midnight snack," I say.

Dad smiles. "When I was your age, I used to get up and make scrambled eggs. Nobody in my family was too surprised when I grew up and opened a restaurant. Maybe you'll be a chef, too."

I'd rather be a chef than a fairy godmother. But I don't have any choice.

Dad stirs the pot of oatmeal and takes a taste. "What do you say we add a little butter and cinnamon?"

Hmm. I wonder if bears like cinnamon?

Bears *love* cinnamon. Katarina sticks her entire snout into the spoonful of oatmeal I brought her and scoffs it down like she hasn't eaten all winter.

Maybe she'll hibernate.

CHAPTER 5

"Give me porridge! Give me. Give me. Give me. PORRIDGE."
I wake up and find Katarina-bear hanging on to my earlobe with her little bear paws and ROARING at me. Talk about morning breath—she has *bear* morning breath!

I bring her a bowl of oatmeal with a side of breath mints, which for some reason she doesn't think is funny.

After school, I'm happy to go to Craft-N-Crunch instead of dealing with Katarina the fairy bear. Including Sunny and Paige, there are nine girls sitting in the art classroom watching Mrs. Fleecy put two heavy plastic tubs down on the table. She smiles at us. "I'm so sorry I'm late! I'm afraid I didn't make Rice Krispies treats."

We all groan. We're less than a minute into Craft-N-Crunch and it's already a disappointment. But then Mrs. Fleecy smiles, opens one of the tubs, and pulls out a plastic bag. "Instead, I made *chocolate chip* Rice Krispies treats!"

Applause erupts as Mrs. Fleecy delivers on the "crunch" of Craft-N-Crunch. I love this club!

"It's a new recipe I'm trying for next month's school carnival. If I say so myself, they're scrumptious!" Mrs. Fleecy reaches into the other tub and pulls out boxes of beads and spools of wire. "I thought we'd start with jewelry making. You can never have too much bling."

Then I have a great idea. I ask, "Mrs. Fleecy? Do we have to make *jewelry*?"

"Goodness, no! These two containers have everything but the kitchen sink in them!"

Half an hour later, eight girls have made eight sparkly neck-laces, and I've made one sparkly fairy bed. I'm hoping that when I give it to Katarina, she'll forgive me for the whole bear thing.

To make the bed, I started with a tiny cardboard box. I cut it down on three sides to make a headboard, padded the bottom with cotton balls, and covered the cotton with red satin. Finally, I glued beads and glitter to the outside. I think it looks awesome.

Mrs. Fleecy holds it up for all the girls to see. "Look what Lacey made! An itsy-bitsy bed!" She hands it back to me. "It must be for a special doll."

"She's special, all right."

I pack the bed in Bubble Wrap, place it in my backpack, and hope Katarina likes my craftsmanship. It's a lot better than a jewelry box.

When Craft-N-Crunch is over, we walk down the hallway and past Room 102, the smelly classroom near the Dumpsters. Inside, Martin is sitting all alone beneath the whiteboard, where he's drawn a design for a jetpack. At least I think it's a design for a jetpack. It kind of looks like a stick figure with Twizzlers strapped to his back.

"Hi, Martin," Sunny says.

Martin leaps to his feet excitedly. "Welcome, welcome, welcome to the Future Flyers Club!"

He reaches into a big shopping bag. "As charter members, you get this great stuff! It's swag that will put swagger in your step!" Almost before we know what's happened, we're holding Future Flyers T-shirts and refrigerator magnets and coffee mugs and baseball caps and bumper stickers and pens that write in four colors.

"Thanks, Martin, but—" I start to say.

"I know exactly what you're thinking. 'How am I ever going to get all this great stuff home?' Problem solved! Tote bags!" And he hands Sunny, Paige, and me promotional Future Flyers bags.

"This is so cool," Sunny says.

"I'm really happy you guys changed your minds about joining the club," Martin says. "Have snacks!" He holds up a platter of cheese, crackers, and gummy worms. "I hope you brought your leaf blowers. We have a lot of work to do!"

Martin looks so happy and hopeful that I feel terrible telling him the truth. "We're not here for your club. We were just walking by."

"*Oh,*" Martin says. "That's okay. But keep your promotional gifts, and tell your friends. Not many people signed up for Future Flyers, but I think it's a publicity problem. I need to get the word out."

Paige looks around the empty room. "Didn't anybody come?"

"I'm expecting Ura Soser to be here any minute now."

"Who's Ura Soser?" Paige asks.

"I don't know, but she was the only one who signed up." He shows us his clipboard, and I peer at the name, scribbled sloppily in blue ink. Oh, poor Martin. It doesn't say "Ura Soser" at all. I take the clipboard away and put it on the table, upside down.

I wink at Paige, "You know Ura. She's in science class." Then I wink again—which Martin sees. (I should have stopped with just one.)

He turns the clipboard around and looks at it again. "Oh. It's not 'Ura Soser.' It's 'U R A Loser.'" He smiles a crooked smile. "It's kind of clever when you think about it." Martin hears footsteps approaching the door. "Hark! I think I hear a Future Flyer!"

But it's not a Future Flyer. It's Principal Conehurst. He's tall, and shiny-bald, and has a beard; it's like his hair has moved from the top of his head to the bottom of his chin. Principal Conehurst puts a hand on the light switch. "So have you people invented the low-cost jetpack yet?" He says it with a smile that shows he thinks the whole idea is so impossible, it's cute. I bet if he *really* thought Martin was inventing a jetpack, he would shut the whole show down for safety reasons. There's no way a principal would let kids zip around with leaf blower rockets strapped to their backs.

But Martin doesn't see that the principal is humoring him. "We're in the design stage, but I'm sure we'll have a working prototype in a month or less!"

"Well, I'm looking forward to taking the first one out for a spin myself," the principal says, still smiling.

Martin shakes his head. "You weigh too much!"

Principal Conehurst flips off the light and waves us toward the door. "Time to shut things down here. Wrap up the club meeting."

"Oh, we're not in the club," Paige says.

Principal Conehurst looks surprised. "So who is?"

Martin raises his hand. "I am."

"And who else?"

"Umm . . ."

"Clubs have to have at least five students—it's a Lincolnite rule," Principal Conehurst explains. "And the last day for sign-ups is Friday."

Martin gulps. "You mean Friday next week?"

"No, I mean Friday tomorrow. Five students or no club." He sounds a little grouchy about it. Martin probably shouldn't have mentioned that he weighed too much.

But Martin stays confident. "No problem!"

As we walk out of school together, Paige asks Martin what we're all thinking. "How, exactly, do you plan on getting five kids in your club by tomorrow?"

"I don't know." Martin suddenly turns to me and says, "Tell the truth, Lacey. Why don't people want to be in my club? I've been handing out T-shirts and magnets all day, but no one came to the meeting."

That's a question I don't want to answer. "Why are you asking me?"

"Sunny is too nice to tell me the truth, and Paige is one of the popular kids who would never join my club anyway. Of anyone I know, you're the one who's most statistically average."

"Thanks a lot!"

"I mean average in a good way! *Why* don't you want to be in the Future Flyers club?"

I hesitate, trying to come up with a nice way to say what I think. But I can't.

Martin gives me a nod of encouragement. "It's okay, Lacey. You can be honest."

"Ahh . . ."

"Please. You're doing me a favor. Nothing you can say will hurt my feelings."

I can't hold the truth back any longer. I blurt it out: "Your club is *boring!*"

Martin looks like I just stabbed him in the heart, and maybe a couple of other places too. I *have* hurt his feelings.

"Lacey!" Paige shrieks. "I can't believe you said that!"

Martin looks at her hopefully. "So you don't think it's boring?"

Paige, looking cornered, says, "Well . . ."

"So you think it's boring, too. But it's about jetpacks! People love jetpacks!"

"*Well* . . ." Paige continues. "Sure, people love jetpacks . . . but building them out of leaf blowers just sounds kind of crazy."

"The biggest discoveries all sounded crazy. People thought cars were crazy, and airplanes were crazy. . . ."

"But leaf blower jetpacks *are* crazy," Paige says.

Martin turns to Sunny, who pretends to be completely

★ 33 ★

fascinated by a poster on the bulletin board about the proper way to sneeze. "How interesting! I never knew you were supposed to sneeze into your elbow. That doesn't even seem possible. Let's all try it!"

Martin steps in front of the sneeze flyer. "Sunny, I need to know. Do you think the Future Flyers Club sounds crazy and boring?"

"Uh, no, it doesn't sound crazy, exactly. And boring can be nice sometimes. A lot of people love boring! If my grandma lived near here, she'd be in your club for sure!" Sunny always means well, but geez. That didn't sound any better than what Paige and I said.

Martin stares at all of us, offended. Then he pulls himself together. "It's not boring! It's exciting, and I'll prove it!"

Martin leaves without saying another word.

Sunny looks unhappy. "We hurt his feelings."

"We just told him the truth," Paige says.

"And that's what hurt his feelings!" Sunny runs after him. "Martin! Wait up!"

I don't care what she says to him—there's no way she's going to make the Future Flyers Club seem like a good, fun, uncrazy, nonboring idea.

I feel totally confident saying this. After all, I'm statistically average.

CHAPTER

6

There's a new KEEP OUT sign on my bedroom door, written in scrawly handwriting—as if a little bear wrote it—and underlined three times in three jagged scratches. The door is locked again.

"Katarina! Let me in!" I whisper, hoping Mom doesn't hear me.

The doorknob unlocks. I turn the handle and wonder what I'll find on the other side. Will it be a room fit for a bear? And what would that look like? A forest with salmon streams and beehives and picnic baskets to raid?

But it's not a forest.

It's an empty white room with one small, white pillow in the middle of the white floor. Katarina sits on top of the pillow with her eyes closed and her bare bear legs crossed in a yoga pose.

"What is all this?" I ask.

"It's minimalist. Very soothing. And I need soothing! I've had a hard day!" Katarina opens her left eye and peers at me. "A fairy godmother needs to be calm and serene at all times." She begins to chant in a droning voice, "I am calm. I am a petal floating in a stream. I am a cloud drifting through the sky. I am not letting the ineptitude of my student affect my inner peace."

Katarina manages to be insulting even when she's being serene.

"I promise to get the spell right tonight."

"I'll do my own spells, thank you. You're not to be trusted."

I'm about to argue that yes, I am. But wait—this is good! "Well, maybe you *should* be the one who gets up at midnight. You seem to feel beary strongly about it."

The "beary" part was pushing it a little too far—she growls at me.

Before Katarina has a chance to start yelling, Mom walks in with an armload of laundry.

I freeze. OMG! She's going to see what Katarina's done to the room! Worse, she's going to see Katarina! She's going to freak out or scream or faint! Probably all three!

Mom doesn't do any of these. She walks over to where Katarina's sitting and puts down the clothes. The laundry floats two feet above the ground, kind of where my bed would be if it were still there. Katarina sits under the levitating laundry, totally unconcerned. This is *weird*.

"Do you have any more homework to do before dinner?"

Mom asks, just as calm as if my room looks the same as always.

Then Julius runs in and jumps on top of the pile of floating laundry. Just like Mom, he acts as if there's nothing different about the room. Feeling like I'm going insane, I finally manage to say, "Homework? Homework . . . I'm doing it!"

"Good." When Mom walks out of the room, I close the door behind her and turn back to Katarina. "What just happened? She didn't see anything!"

"One isn't a fairy godmother for hundreds of years without learning a few tricks of the trade. Only you and I can see the spells I'm putting on your room. As far as everyone else is concerned, all of your putrid furniture is still here."

"But why didn't she see *you*?"

"Since your mother still sees your furniture, she can't see me because I'm under the bed."

"So if my stuff is all still here, does that mean I can sleep on my bed?" I run over and plop down on it—and tumble backward onto the floor. From my backpack, there's the sound of something breaking.

Katarina smirks. "No. As far as *you're* concerned, your furniture is gone." Then she closes her eyes and chants, "I am a petal floating in a stream. . . ."

I peer into my backpack and see that the bed I made for Katarina is smashed flat. Next week in Craft-N-Crunch, I'm going to have to start all over again.

Sigh.

As Katarina chants, sheets of paper magically appear and float around her like petals. I glance at a sheet as it floats by and see the words *Only jerks shirk their homework.*

"Hey!" I say. "These are my pages!"

"You turned them in to me, so now they're mine. And they're not good enough! Your handwriting was atrocious!"

"It was atrocious because my hand almost fell off! *You* try writing that a thousand times."

"I don't need to, because I'm the teacher and you're the student." She nods at the swirling pages, and they fall to the floor at my feet. "They're not good enough. Do it again. Only this time, I want you to write it *five* thousand times!"

This is so unfair! Katarina is the worst teacher in the world. I'm just being punished because she's too lazy to teach me anything. No matter how many times I write "Only jerks shirk their homework," I'm not going to learn a thing from it.

Katarina says, "You're dawdling! So now I want to see it written out *ten* thousand times!"

The pages near my feet turn blank; everything I wrote yesterday has been erased.

I'm so mad that I feel like either stomping or crying. I fumble in my backpack for a pencil, but by mistake, the first thing I grab is my wand. I'm about to put it down when I think, If Katarina wants ten thousand sentences now, I'll *give* her ten thousand now!

Raising the little wand above my head, I chant, "Write my homework again, a thousand times ten!" When I toss the spell at my pencil, it floats up in the air and then zooms down and starts gliding across the pages almost faster than I can see. *Only jerks shirk their homework* appears over and over again, in beautiful handwriting.

As the pages fill with words, I deliberately don't look at Katarina—but I bet she's sooo *mad*. When the pencil finally stops, it's so hot from all the writing that a little wisp of smoke rises out of it.

I pick up the pages and say, "Ten thousand sentences, just like you wanted!" I expect Katarina to be glaring at me. But instead, there's a trace of a grin on her lips.

"*Now* you've learned something," she says. "It certainly took you long enough!"

"What did I learn?"

Katarina just stares at me, waiting for an answer. She finally sighs and says, "If you know when to use it, magic is an excellent tool. And this was a good time to use it."

"Why didn't you just tell me that in the first place?"

"Because I'm a wonderful teacher, that's why!"

Wonderful isn't exactly the word I'd use for her.

CHAPTER 7

"Paige Harrington is today's fashion-*do!*" Makayla has cornered me and Paige in the cafeteria line to interview us for next Monday's webcast, while her cheerleader buddy Taylor Margolis acts as cameraperson. "Good work, Paige," Makayla says. "Those cute shoes you're wearing make even an everyday drop-waist jersey dress look pulled together! And now, drumroll, please."

Taylor makes a fake drumroll sound.

Makayla points at me. "Today's fashion-*don't* is Lacey Unger-Ware!" Taylor turns the camera my way, panning up from my tennis shoes to my slightly tangled hair. (Katarina made me late this morning.) Then Makayla looks back at the camera and says, "Need I say more?"

And this is one of the many reasons why Makayla is not my favorite person. Katarina *did* say that magic is an excellent tool—a tool I could use to turn Makayla into my least favorite animal, the Pacific banana slug. (Look it up if you're brave. They're gross.) I'm about to pull out my wand but stop myself. After all, I am on camera. Plus I'd have to carry the Makayla-slug around all day so nobody squishes her, which would be disgusting.

Across the cafeteria, I see Sunny poking her head in through the double doors at the back of the room. Then she puts her fingers in her mouth and whistles her insanely loud whistle. Every single kid looks at her; when Sunny whistles, people notice.

Sunny calls, "Ladies and gentlemen! Please join me in the courtyard for a demonstration from Martin Shembly's soon-to-be-famous Future Flyers!"

"Do you know anything about this?" Paige asks me.

I shake my head. "Sunny didn't mention it in homeroom. But she did keep smiling about something."

Makayla starts pushing people aside to get out the door. "Breaking news! Out of my way! Makayla Brandice on the scene."

Paige and I—along with all the other kids from the cafeteria—hurry outside to see what's going on. It seems like half the school is out here. I don't know what Martin's got planned, but it better be good.

Makayla talks into the camera. "Hello, Lincoln! I'm here in the cafeteria courtyard waiting for some kind of demonstration from Martin Shembly. I'm sure it's going to be *good*." And then she gives an evil smirk at the camera. Maybe I *should* turn her into a Pacific banana slug.

Makayla walks over to Sunny and asks in her fake-reporter voice, "Sandy Varden, what do you know about what Martin is planning?"

"My name is Sunny."

"Whatever. What is Martin planning?"

"I don't know, but he says it's going to be cool!"

Martin's voice booms overhead. "ONE SMALL STEP FOR A MAN . . ."

Where is he? Everyone in the courtyard looks around, confused. "Up here!" Martin says.

Along with everyone else, I look up and see Martin high in the air, clinging to the side of the school's old water tower.

The water tower is a historic symbol of Lincoln Middle School. The big tank at the top is painted to look like Abraham Lincoln's black stovepipe hat, and there's a flat part at the base of the tank that looks like the hat's brim. The school stopped using the water tower a long time ago, and the school board talked about tearing it down, but the students got so upset that the tower stayed.

It might be old and rusty, but the Lincoln tower has been on the cover of every yearbook since even before my mom and dad went to school here.

Martin repeats, "One small step for a man; one giant leap for mankind. This is the future of transportation." Now I notice he's wearing gray coveralls and a yellow bicycle helmet—and there's a leaf blower strapped to his back. He shouts, "Jetpacks for everyone! Join the Future Flyers Club and do THIS." He pushes a button, and the leaf blower roars to life. Then he steps off the edge of the water tower. I gasp, and everyone else in the courtyard does, too.

Instead of falling, Martin glides smoothly toward the ground. Wow! He actually made a jetpack!

Makayla talks loudly to Taylor's camera: "Exclusive report! Martin Shembly can fly!"

Scott Dearden shouts, "Way to go, Martin!"

WHIRRRRR! Martin glides even closer. But then I suddenly see that he's not really using the leaf blower to fly—he's on a zip line. The high end of the line is attached to the brim of Lincoln's hat.

Martin lands perfectly on the ground and looks proudly at the crowd. Even if it wasn't a jetpack—that was kind of amazing. And I'm not the only one who thinks so. The kids in the courtyard swarm around him, smiling and excited.

"This was only a demonstration," Martin says. "So join the Future Flyers and help me turn leaf blower jetpacks into reality!" He waves a sign-up sheet.

Makayla has a sneer on her face. "Breaking news! Fartin'

Martin attempts to punk the entire school! This reporter never believed it for a minute!"

Because of Makayla, the mood in the courtyard shifts in a split second, and Martin tries to get everyone excited again. "I wasn't trying to punk anybody! I was just showing how cool our club will be!" Martin keeps waving the sign-up sheet, but nobody takes it from him. Makayla's sneer is like a force field stopping anyone from moving toward him.

But one person is immune to Makayla's force field: Scott Dearden. He pushes his way through the crowd. "That was *awesome*! Do you really think we can make a jetpack?"

Martin nods eagerly. "Yes, we can!"

Scott writes his name at the top of the list. "Count me in!"

Next Dylan Hernandez, one of the coolest kids on the basketball team, walks over and adds his name to the list, too. A moment later there's a line of kids excited to sign up for the club. Martin did it! He grins, ear to ear.

Sunny rushes up to me and Paige. "Isn't this *great*?"

I'm just starting to nod yes when there's a loud cracking sound from the water tower. We look up just in time to see Lincoln's hat brim cracking apart. The pieces start to crash to the ground, and the kids in the courtyard gasp.

Martin looks horrified. "We can fix that," he yells. "It wasn't structural! Nothing to worry about."

Groaning and creaking sounds rumble from the old tank.

"*Probably* nothing to worry about," Martin says.

Rusty, sludgy water starts to drip from the bottom of the tank.

"Still nothing to worry about . . . but RUN!" Martin shouts. "Run! Run! RUN!"

WHOOSH!

The tank splits apart like a dam breaking. Icky, dirty water spews all over the courtyard. Makayla, who's now the closest to the legs of the water tower, is swept off her feet. Taylor manages to scramble away—it's every cheerleader for herself.

Kids shriek and run as more water floods down into the courtyard, turning over the furniture and toppling garbage cans. Sunny, Paige, and I jump up on a planter and try not to get soaked.

"This way, everybody!" Martin shouts. He pulls open the door to the school's basement—and then there's one final wave of rusty, sludgy, gross water from the tower. He gets knocked off his feet, too, and disappears down the steps.

Sunny, Paige, and I all scream at once. (And that's a really, really loud scream.)

But a moment later, Martin reappears, covered in slime and a lot of purple and gold crepe paper streamers. He looks like a soggy homecoming float.

"All the stuff for the school carnival is down there," Paige says. "Everything will be *ruined*!"

The cafeteria door slams open, and Principal Conehurst splashes his way out into the courtyard. "What happened here? Is anybody hurt?" Martin's going to be in *such* big trouble.

Martin holds up his soaked sign-up sheet in triumph. "Principal Conehurst, I'm really sorry. But look—I have six new members for the Future Flyers Club!"

CHAPTER 8

Thanks to Martin, we have the most exciting lunchtime our school has ever seen. Fire trucks arrive to pump out the water. Ambulances arrive—sirens blaring, lights flashing—in case anybody got hurt. (Nobody did. For a little while, the EMTs thought Makayla had two black eyes, but then they realized it was smeared mascara.) Even the police show up. (More sirens! More flashing lights!)

Martin is hauled off to the office, and for the rest of us, school is canceled.

As Sunny, Paige, and I sit outside on the school's front steps waiting for Martin to come out, we stare up at what's left of the water tower. The legs are still standing, but the tank at the top is almost gone. There are just a couple of wiggly pieces of metal up there to show where it used to be.

"I know Martin didn't mean to wreck it," Sunny says. "But I loved our Lincoln hat. No other school had one."

"And now we don't either," Paige says.

"Uh-oh," Sunny says, watching a car pull into the parking lot. "It's Martin's mom and dad. They look mad."

They don't just look mad, they *sound* mad. As they walk toward the front door, we can hear them arguing:

"I told you he didn't have time for clubs! But no, you let him tinker in the basement instead of practicing the violin," Martin's mom says.

Martin's dad shakes his head. "I didn't know he was going to destroy the school!"

They disappear inside, the doors slamming behind them.

"He's in sooo much trouble," I say.

Sunny and Paige nod in agreement. "Do you think we should wait for him?" Sunny asks. "Maybe we can talk to his parents."

"*I'm* not talking to his parents!" Paige says.

I'm glad Paige said that, because I don't want to talk to his parents, either.

Sunny pauses. "Maybe we *should* let them calm down a little."

"Like for a year," I say.

"Or two," Paige says. "So what do we do now—go home? What a waste of a free afternoon."

"We could go to the mall and get Martin a sympathy card," Sunny says.

I don't think they make SORRY YOU DESTROYED YOUR SCHOOL cards, but I still think the mall's a fun idea. Paige jumps to her feet. "Let's go!"

The three of us walk away from the school, but when we reach the corner, something strange happens. My shoes suddenly freeze to the sidewalk.

"Come on, Lacey!" Paige says.

I struggle to lift my foot, but it won't budge, not even an inch. "I'm trying!"

"What's wrong with you?" Sunny asks.

"I can't move!"

Sunny and Paige lean down and tug at my feet, but it doesn't help.

"Did you do something with your magic wand?" Paige asks.

"No. It's in my pocket."

All at once, my shoes turn around and start walking, and so I have to walk, too. "I can't stop!" I wail.

Sunny and Paige grab my arms, and my shoes kick them. The girls both leap away.

"I'm sorry! It's not me!"

The shoes start running me in the direction of my house. "I'll text you!" I yell back at the girls as they vanish into the distance.

When my shoes have trotted me halfway home, I see Scott on the corner doing spins on his unicycle. "Hey, Lacey!"

"Hey, Scott." It's going to seem rude if I run right past him, so I try to stop and run in place for a moment. But the shoes keep dragging me down the sidewalk. "I'm . . . uh . . . jogging! I want to be in shape for the Uni-Cyclones."

"That's great!" Scott pedals alongside me, hopping on and off the curb with the unicycle.

"You're really good!" I say as my shoes sprint me along.

"Thanks. I'm hoping our whole club can go to the Uni-Convention next spring."

"Uni-Convention?" You'd think I'd be out of breath from all the running I'm doing, but I think the shoes are doing most of the work.

"It's in Kingston every year. There are unicycles everywhere! If the school carnival has a good turnout next month, we can get money from the school fund and go." He suddenly thinks of something. "The water got into the school basement where the carnival supplies are. Do you think a lot of stuff got wrecked?"

"I hope not," I say.

We reach my house, and my shoes sprint up the porch steps while Scott unicycles in place on the sidewalk.

"I guess I better go," I say.

"Okay. Lacey, I was wondering something. . . ."

I wonder what he's wondering. To try to slow the shoes down,

I sit on the porch rail and let the shoes run in the air. It probably looks a little crazy, so I say, "It's always good to cool down for a while after a run. What did you want to talk about?"

The shoes seem to realize I'm struggling against them, so they (and my feet) air-run even harder. It's all I can do not to fall off the porch rail.

Scott stammers, "I was kind of wondering if you . . . you and I . . . we could go to a—"

Whump! My shoes pedal so hard that I fall backward off the porch rail into the bushes.

"Lacey!" Scott calls over the railing. "Are you all right?"

"Fine! Fine!" I say as my feet kick the side of the house.

As Scott reaches into the bushes to help me up, there's a booming voice from inside: "LACEY UNGER-WARE! YOU GET IN HERE THIS INSTANT!"

It's Katarina, but Scott doesn't know that. "Uh-oh—your mom sounds mad."

"I better go in."

"YOU'RE DARN RIGHT YOU BETTER GO IN!"

CHAPTER

9

The shoes march me right to my bedroom.

Only it's not my bedroom. It's a classroom, complete with a chalkboard and narrow wooden desks. It looks like something out of an old movie. The shoes yank me to a desk at the front of the room, and I topple into it. A thick book slams down onto the desk, ready for me to study.

Katarina flies up to me. "You were lollygagging at school!"

"I was not lollygagging. I don't even know what lollygagging means."

"It means goofing off."

"I was not!" Okay, that was a lie. But there's no reason that Katarina needs to know school was canceled.

Suddenly, my feet start tapping and I can't stop them. TAP TAP, tap TAP, tap TAP tap tap, tap TAP tap tap. "What are they doing?" I ask.

Katarina cocks her head, listening to the sounds. "Morse

code, of course. Your shoes say you were going to the mall!"

I look down at my sneakers. "You're a couple of tattletales! See if I wear you again."

"Don't blame your shoes," Katarina says. "It's not *their* fault you were lollygagging."

"School got canceled!"

"But magic lessons didn't."

"That's not fair! And you stopped Scott in the middle of asking whatever he was going to ask me!"

Katarina rolls her eyes, which makes me even madder.

I cross my arms and glare at her. "*And* I should get some part of my bedroom for myself! Is it going to be like this forever?"

Katarina says, "Do you think I'm happy about this? I used to have a life, and friends, and lovely parties to go to. Now I've just got you, this room, and your detestable cat! It's all too, too, much." She puts her head in her hands and sobs, her little shoulders heaving and her wings drooping.

Geez. This is *really* not fair. This was supposed to be about me, and now it's about her. Still . . . she does have a point.

"Don't cry," I finally say. "We're stuck with each other. I'll study if you'll split the room with me fifty-fifty."

Katarina looks up at me with red, puffy eyes. "Seventy-thirty."

Okay. This *is* about me. "Fifty-fifty!"

"Sixty-forty, plus you read whatever I tell you to read this weekend."

I look at Katarina's sad, smeary face, and I don't have the heart to argue anymore. "Deal."

"Start reading," Katarina says.

I flip open the book on the desk in front of me. At least it's just one. Maybe I can read it this afternoon and have the weekend free.

Then there's a rumbling sound, and an old wooden library cart rolls up to me. It's crammed with dusty books about fairy godmothering.

If I knew Morse code, I'd be tapping out "Help me!"

That cart of books is *huge*. There's no way I can read all of those in a weekend! Hmmm . . . Katarina said it was okay to use magic. But how can magic help me read?

I think about doing a spell that makes all the facts from all the books get zapped into my head. Probably a bad idea: there are at least a hundred ways fact zapping could go wrong, many of them involving my brain popping like a balloon.

Maybe Sunny and Paige would read some of them and give me book reports. But even if they would be nice enough to do that, there's still too much here to read. I need about ten book reporters. But where would I get all those people?

I know!

Right outside my window, there's a trail of ants walking by like they always do. A couple of months ago, I did a spell that turned an ant into a little footman—footmen are personal servants and very handy. If a footman can help polish jewelry (which is what my footman did), he can write a book report.

Raising my wand, I chant, "I need many book reports, so send me footmen in shorts!"

Katarina shudders. "Ugh! You've made some bad rhymes before, but that one's the worst!"

Too late; I've already tossed the spell. There are flashes of sparkly pink light, and a dozen three-inch-tall men wearing white wigs and satin shorts appear on my windowsill. They all shout, "Milady! What can I read for you?" in their high, squeaky voices.

I go to the library cart and put twelve books on twelve desks. Then I put a footman next to each book and say, "Everybody, read your book and then tell me what it's about."

I'm so smart.

Two hours later, I'm thinking, I'm so stupid, as twelve little footmen all simultaneously tell me what they've read.

"And then, in 1542, Griselda Greenbriar said . . ."

"The prince was so happy that he gave Adelaide a solid-gold house. The settee was gold, the fireplace was gold, the bed was gold. And you'll never guess what the toilet was made of. . . ."

"By the fall of 1756, her split ends had become unmanageable, and her fairy godmother . . . Oh, wait, I forgot to tell you that early in 1755 . . ."

There are nine more book reports going on at once. None

of them make much sense—they remind me of when Madison tries to tell me about cartoons she watched, and she gets everything mixed up. And with all the footmen talking at the same time, I can't understand anything.

"Quiet! Quiet!" I plead.

The footmen ignore me and keep on blabbering.

I look over at Katarina, hoping for some teacherly help. She's sitting on a desk reading another fashion magazine, and she's wearing fluffy earmuffs over her ears to block out the sound.

On the chalkboard behind her, Katarina has written, *Just because you can use magic doesn't mean you should.*

Now she tells me!

The little footmen talk in my ear until midnight. I don't learn a thing.

CHAPTER 10

By the time I walk to school Monday morning (and believe me, I'm wearing different shoes), I've read so many fairy godmother autobiographies that my brain hurts. Since the footmen weren't helpful at all, I had to read the old-fashioned way. With my eyes. My burning, tired eyes. I'd tell you some titles, but the books were all about people you've never heard of helping other people you've never heard of.

Sunny joins me along the way. "Where were you this weekend? I texted you about a million times."

"Katarina took my phone because she wanted me to study. What did I miss?"

"Martin's mom called my mom and told her I needed to leave Martin alone."

"That's weird! Why?"

"Mrs. Shembly said Martin needs to concentrate on his violin and stay out of trouble."

"You weren't the one who got him into trouble! You guys weren't even spending that much time together."

"That's what my mom said. And she said a few other things, too, before she hung up on Mrs. Shembly."

I *love* Sunny's mom. "Are you upset about it?"

"No. I'm just upset for Martin. He doesn't have that many friends."

I think about what she just said, and I'm sure Sunny is right. These days, Martin needs all the friends he can get.

When we reach the school, we see a new chain link fence around what's left of the old water tower. The legs look *so* bare without the Lincoln stovepipe hat on top of them.

Mrs. Neff, our homeroom teacher, tells us to go straight to the gym for an assembly. This has never happened before, at least not that I can remember.

"You don't think the assembly's going to be about Martin, do you?" Sunny whispers in my ear.

"I don't think it's going to be about Martin—I *know* it is."

After we sit down in the bleachers in the gym, Principal Conehurst walks to the podium. Usually before an assembly, everybody's giggling and joking. But today he looks so serious that all the students are quiet.

Principal Conehurst switches on the microphone. "Good

morning, students. I didn't want rumors spreading, so I would like to talk to you all directly about the incident on Friday and its consequences."

Ooh. An adult talking about "consequences" is never a good thing.

"I've been meeting all weekend with the school board, and there are three things I need to tell you. First, it was decided that, since the water tower was so severely damaged, it will be torn down."

There are unhappy murmurs from the kids, and Principal Conehurst raises his hands for silence. "I know the water tower is a symbol of the school, but there's simply not enough money in the budget to repair something that hasn't been used in years."

Yikes. The kids are definitely going to blame Martin for this. I look around to see how he's reacting, but I don't see him anywhere.

Principal Conehurst says, "The next decision was about the school carnival. All the carnival supplies were stored in the school basement, where we had severe flood damage. Unfortunately, the school's insurance policy doesn't *cover* flood damage. So I'm very sorry to tell you that this year's carnival is going to have to be canceled."

Now there aren't just unhappy murmurs from the crowd—there are groans and moans. The carnival isn't fancy, but it's fun and everyone looks forward to it. There are games and prizes and booths. At least there *were* games and prizes and booths, until

Martin decided it was a good idea to zip-line off the water tower.

Principal Conehurst taps on the microphone. "Quiet, everyone. I'm almost finished. The third thing I need to tell you also isn't very pleasant. The carnival raised money for many of the after-school clubs' activities. So, for this year at least, all you Lincolnites will need to pinch your pennies. No new supplies will be bought, and all field trips will be canceled."

OMG! This is horrible. I'm in five clubs! That's five field trips I won't get to go on!

Makayla leaps to her feet. "Principal Conehurst! I can still go to the Online News Association banquet, right?"

Principal Conehurst shakes his head. "There just won't be the money for that, Makayla. I'm very sorry."

Makayla's eyes turn fierce. "This is all Martin Shembly's fault! He's wrecked everything! The water tower! The carnival! The clubs! And what are you going to do about it!"

"Makayla, this isn't the place—"

"Yes, it is! He should be expelled! Or arrested! Or both!"

"Miss Brandice, sit down right now!"

Ooh. She got *Miss*-ed. Even Makayla is no match for that, so she sits back down on the bleachers.

Principal Conehurst looks out at all of us sternly. "I understand how disappointed everyone is, but I want to make one thing perfectly clear. I won't tolerate any bullying. Any reprisals against Martin Shembly will result in suspension or worse. This

is the end of the assembly. Now go to your first period classes."

Everyone in the gym starts talking at once. The one word I keep hearing is "Martin."

And for Martin, that's not a good thing.

Sunny turns to me. "Where is he?"

As Sunny and I walk to first period, we see Mrs. Fleecy behind her counter in the school office.

"I'm going to find out what's going on," Sunny says, and I follow her as she goes up to the counter. "Is Martin okay?" Sunny asks.

"That's confidential, dear."

"I have to know! He's my friend—except now his mother won't let me talk to him." Sunny's eyes shine, and I can tell she's trying not to cry.

Mrs. Fleecy leans forward and pats Sunny's hand. She says in a low voice, "He'll be all right. He's suspended for a week, and then he's got three months of campus cleanup duty. It could have been a lot worse."

Ugh. Campus cleanup is this new thing that Principal Conehurst started, where instead of just sitting around in detention, you have to spend your time helping the janitor empty garbage cans and mop stuff up.

Maybe it could have been worse, but three months of that is still really, really bad.

CHAPTER 11

When Martin returns to school a week later, he's gone from being sort-of-invisible to being the biggest outcast in Lincoln Middle School's history. People *hate* him. If it were me, I'd spend all my time hiding. But Martin can't hide—he's got campus cleanup duty.

I'm worried that Martin will get beaten up, but that doesn't happen. Instead, people "accidentally" trip him, step on his feet, and knock his books out of his hands. People always tell him *sorry*, but they don't mean it. They're mad at Martin, and they're letting him know it.

Makayla, who's got to be absolutely furious about losing her trip to the news banquet, never once says the words "Martin Shembly" on her morning webcasts. But one night she posts a video on her "Makayla Unscripted" Web site. (She has a *script* for the webcasts? Who knew!)

She talks into the camera. "Hello, Lincoln Middle School. This is Makayla Brandice, speaking from her heart." (She has a heart? Who *knew*!) "I'm worried about Martin Shembly. I don't think he's very happy at Lincoln Middle School. I've found a number of wonderful military academies and correctional boarding schools that might be perfect for him. Martin, if you're listening, I'll post them on my site. If I were you, my very top choice might be the Grindavik Academy in Chile. It's safe and secure, and I'm sure that live volcano is nothing to worry about."

Makayla pauses like she's thinking deep thoughts. "But while Martin is still with us, fellow students, remember to be extra, extra, extra tidy in the halls. We wouldn't want to make poor Martin's life harder with spills, and gum, and trash, would we?"

Wow. Makayla is sneaky. She's pretending to be nice, but she's really sending out a not-so-secret message about how to make Martin's life even more miserable.

A lot of kids must have watched Makayla's video because Martin's campus cleanup the next day is the worst ever. He has to scrape gum off the hallway floors, pick up overturned trash cans in the boys' bathroom, and mop up mud from the gym floor.

After school, Sunny and I peer into the cafeteria and see Martin by himself looking at gallons of grape soda spilled on the floor. "Martin's life stinks," Sunny says.

"Martin's life *really* stinks. I wish I could help him."

"Can't you just do a little magic for him?" Sunny begs.

"Well . . . I guess so."

So when Martin leaves the cafeteria to empty one of the many overflowing trash cans, I pull out my wand and chant, "Martin is needy, so mop be speedy." Then I toss the spell at the mop that Martin has left behind.

There's a flash, and the mop lurches up and wipes the cafeteria floor in a squeaky, squishy blur. Just as Martin comes back, I grab the mop, which wiggles in my hand like it wants to go clean the entire school. Martin stares at the floor, bewildered.

"Surprise!" Sunny says.

I hold the mop like I've just been pushing it. "We wanted to help out!"

Martin keeps staring at the gleaming floor. "How did you do this so fast?"

"At the restaurant, I learned how to speed clean," I lie. The mop wiggles in my hand again, so I rush toward the door before it gets away from me.

Martin calls, "Hey! I need to put the mop away!"

"We'll do it for you," I say. "You go home! Bye!"

Sunny and I are out the door before Martin can say another word. I put the mop on the floor, and it pulls me along like a super hyper puppy on a leash.

"You've got to make it stop," Sunny says.

"I can't! It'll do this till midnight!"

"But somebody's going to see it!"

She's right. Magic spells can cause as many problems as they solve, at least for me. As the mop yanks me down the hall, I finally get an idea. "Sunny—open your locker."

Sunny runs ahead and turns the combination, but the mop drags me right past in a cleaning frenzy.

"Slow down, mop!" I command, but the mop ignores me. It's heading for the gym and its gigantic floor. Once the mop starts cleaning that place, it's never going to stop. Desperate, I say, "Mop! Go back! Sunny spilled a whole carton of milk in her locker, and it's starting to smell!"

The mop can't resist. I let go of the handle, and it zips back down to Sunny's locker and hops inside. Sunny slams the door, and it's trapped. We can hear it rattling, but there's no way for it to escape.

"Well, the bottom of my locker is going to be really, really clean," Sunny says. "And thank you for helping Martin."

"You're welcome. But I can't help him anymore—Martin's sure to figure out it's magic. From now on he's going to have to do his own mopping."

We hear a frantic *let-me-out!* handle-tapping sound from inside the locker as we leave.

CHAPTER 12

Two fairies zoom up and wag their fingers in my face the second I step inside my room.

One of them is Katarina, who's shouting, "How could you! How could you!"

And the other one is blue-eyed, blue-haired Augustina Oberon. "You stupid girl! Stupid, stupid, stupid!" Augustina is the fairy who, instead of sending me away to the Godmother Academy, decided to let me be homeschooled. (Actually, Katarina blackmailed her into giving me permission. And since Augustina was in Julius's stomach at the time, she went along with it. Long story.)

"Is this about the mop?" I ask. "It'll be fine in Sunny's locker."

"It's not about the mop. It's about the spell bind you just created," Katarina snaps.

"What's a spell bind?"

Augustina flies in front of my face like an angry wasp. "Did you or did you not help one Martin Paganini Shembly with a cleaning spell?"

"His middle name is Paganini? That's so weird!"

Katarina says, "Paganini was a famous violinist and a very nice man. He played me a concerto for my birthday in 1802. I was very young, of course!"

Augustina screeches at us both. "Pay attention, you blithering fools! Katarina, you're the teacher. Supposedly. Explain to your pupil what a spell bind is."

Katarina flies down and lands on my shoulder. "When you don't have a client, and you do a spell to help someone, that spell binds you to them as their fairy godmother."

"But I used spells when I didn't have a client to make you lemon-flavored. And to turn you into the bear."

"Godmother-to-godmother magic doesn't count. You did a spell to help Martin! *It was a spell bind!*"

"AND IT'S SIMPLY NOT ALLOWED!" Augustina shouts. "Fairy godmothers can't go around choosing their clients."

Katarina nods. "If you *could* choose your own clients, everyone would try to bribe you and give you gifts." She gets a faraway expression. "Although gifts are nice. . . ."

Fairy godmothers have so many rules! I shrug. "Sorry! I won't do it again."

Augustina stares at me. "It's too late. Martin Shembly is now your client. This assignment appeared at Fairy Godmother

Central this afternoon." With one flick of her wand, Augustina makes a tiny rectangular piece of paper, half the size of a postage stamp, float in front of my face. "Here is your client's dream. You need to make it come true."

The paper has writing that's so small, I almost have to cross my eyes to read it. The writing says, *Your client is Martin Shembly, and you need to make his life not-stink.*

I'm sort of happy inside. "Martin sure needs a fairy godmother. Maybe my spell bind is accidentally a good thing."

Ow! I get a kick on one side of my neck from Katarina, and on the other side from Augustina. I brush them both off my shoulders and they fall onto my bed.

Augustina glares at Katarina. "Haven't you taught this girl anything?"

Katarina glares right back. "We were getting to the lesson about spell binds next week."

Augustina shouts, "You're a horrible teacher! You should be drummed out of the Godmothers' League." Then the two fairies start kicking each other.

Better than kicking me, I think, and I smile a little at the thought—which Augustina sees. She snaps at me, "You won't be smiling when you hear your punishment."

The smile vanishes from my face. This is going to be something awful, I'm sure. I've said it before and I'll say it again: fairies play rough. "What *kind* of punishment?"

Augustina fluffs her blue hair, enjoying this. "Let's start with your teacher. Since your homeschooling is Katarina's responsibility, if you fail to get Martin his dream by the exact moment of the full moon, Katarina will be exiled to the South Pole without wand or wings."

Katarina shudders. "That means penguins! I hate penguins!"

Augustina gives Katarina a sparkling smile. "I know! Perfect, isn't it?"

"And what about me?" I ask.

"You will be exiled along with your teacher—as her servant. Oh, and of course Martin's life will stink forever. But these things happen."

OMG! That's terrible!

Augustina gives me the same sparkling smile. "Well, Lacey,

you'd better get busy! The full moon will be here before you know it!" She flies toward the door, leaving a trail of electric-blue sparkles that fizzle out on the carpet. Just before she leaves, she flicks her wand at the wall below my Endangered Animals calendar. A dime-sized hole appears, and a cold breeze whistles through. "On the other side of that portal, Antarctica awaits," Augustina says, and then she's gone.

Katarina looks up at me, rubbing her shin where she got kicked. "I hope you're happy! Soon we're both going to be living in an igloo and fighting off penguins."

"They wouldn't really send us to Antarctica, would they?"

"If you'd read the biography of Swettlanda Puck the way you were supposed to, instead of giving it to those silly footmen, you'd know the answer is *eaeyeeeap!*"

"What's that?"

"'Yes' in Penguin."

I sit on the bed next to Katarina, feeling dizzy. "But I don't want to live in an igloo."

"Then you better have Martin squared away by the full moon."

"When is that?"

"Look it up. You're the one with the internal."

When I finally figure out she means Internet, I search for the date on my phone. "The moon is full at 12:34 a.m. on Sunday the twenty-eighth." I count on my fingers. "That's nine days from now. Nine days! Just once I'd like to have a full thirty days to complete a fairy godmother assignment."

"You're the one who got yourself into this mess. It's not the Godmothers' League's fault that you don't have enough time."

"It's not just me in this mess. *We're* in this mess. Tell me how to help Martin!"

Katarina scratches her head. "You do have a point there. All right. The first thing you need to do is—" Then her mouth clamps shut, and though she's clearly struggling to say something, no more sounds come out.

"Katarina! What's wrong?" I ask. A moment later, a little piece of paper comes floating down from the ceiling. I grab it and read it out loud: "Teachers teach and students learn. Lacey Unger-Ware, you must find the answers for yourself. NO CHEATING!"

Another note floats down, and I read it, too. It says, "And tell Katarina I'm WATCHING HER. Love and sparkly kisses, Augustina."

Katarina coughs and her mouth pops again. "I can't help you. But I *can* say I hate that know-it-all fairy!"

I run to the door.

"Where are you going?" she asks.

"If you can't help me, then I need my godmother posse. Come on!"

CHAPTER 13

"**W**hat are you supposed to do?" Paige asks me.

Sunny, Paige, and I sit in Paige's family room eating popcorn. (Paige says there's no problem so big that popcorn won't help.) Katarina perches on the ottoman munching on a single popped kernel; since it's almost as big as her head, she has to hold it in both hands.

I pull out the tiny piece of paper and read out loud, "'Your client is Martin Shembly, and you need to make his life not-stink.'"

"Martin's life *is* pretty stinky," Sunny says.

"But that's so vague! Martin is in middle school! Of course his life stinks," Paige says.

"I've been thinking about it," I say. "A couple of weeks ago, Martin was happy. But now everyone hates him. So I'm thinking what we need to do is make people *not* hate him anymore. It's going to be really hard."

"Ya think?" Katarina says, super sarcastically.

I ignore her and say, "But before we do anything, I have to tell him I'm his fairy godmother. I hate this part—he's never going to believe me! Paige didn't believe me; Sunny's mother didn't believe me; nobody *ever* believes me when I tell them I'm a fairy godmother."

Katarina can't resist rubbing it in. "I never have that problem at all."

"That's because you're three inches tall with butterfly wings and a poufy dress!"

Sunny looks at me, squinting. "What if you used a spell to shrink yourself? Just for when you first meet him."

I shake my head. "It's too dangerous. I could get trapped in a spiderweb. Or I could get blown away by a gust of wind—"

"Or you could get eaten by your cat," Katarina says.

"Julius wouldn't eat me."

"Shall we shrink you down and see?"

Okay, she's probably right. Julius *would* eat me; if I was bug size, I'd be cat food for sure. But instead of admitting that out loud, I repeat, "It's too dangerous. So what else can I do to make Martin believe I'm his fairy godmother?"

Paige, Sunny, and Katarina study me like I'm an exhibit at the natural history museum. Feeling self-conscious, I straighten my T-shirt over my jeans.

"That's it!" Paige shouts.

"What's it?" I ask.

"It's the way you're dressed. Nobody believes you're a fairy godmother because you don't dress like one."

"So what am I supposed to do, dress like Katarina?"

And Paige, Sunny, and I all turn and study the tiny fairy like she's in the natural history museum.

Katarina puts her hands on her hips. "What's wrong with the way I look? I've been on the ten-best-dressed-fairies list for the last three centuries. Have any of you?"

Paige leans forward and touches the fabric of Katarina's sparkly dress. Katarina slaps her finger. "No popcorn hands!"

"Lacey, do you think you could copy the dress?" Paige asks me.

"Why?"

"If you showed up at Martin's place wearing a dress like this, at least you'd *look* like a fairy godmother."

Katarina seems dubious, but Sunny is enthusiastic. "And then do a little magic, and Martin will believe you're a fairy godmother, no problem!"

This makes sense. This makes a *lot* of sense. I pull out my wand and chant, "No need to guess! I'll copy this dress!" I toss the spell in a swishing motion, and magic sparkles swirl in the air. A moment later a miniature gown, exactly like Katarina's, falls to the floor. I pick up the tiny dress with my thumb and forefinger and stare at it. "Well, it *looks* like a perfect copy, all right."

Katarina snorts. "Amateur."

Hoping my next spell works better, I chant, "Copy her dress, but my size, not less!" and swish the wand again. The same magic sparkles swirl, but this time a dress big enough for me appears.

Sunny applauds, and we all go over to look at it.

"I never realized how beautiful Katarina's dress is," Paige says. "Look at the embroidery and the jewels—"

"And cloth of gold, and crystals from Paris, and pearls from a lagoon in Bali," Katarina adds. "I designed it myself."

I'm feeling smug about making such a perfect copy. Then I try to pick up the dress. Yikes! It weighs a ton! "Katarina, how can you wear this?"

"With style and panache, of course."

Sunny struggles to lift up one of the puffy sleeves. "Maybe it will be better after you put it on."

It's a thought. Sunny and Paige help me squirm into the gown. I've heard that firemen's gear is really heavy, but I bet it's nothing compared to Katarina's six-ton gown. I stand with my knees quivering as I try to balance.

"How is it?" Sunny asks.

"Not too bad," I say. Then . . . WHOMP! I topple over backward onto the couch. I can tell I'm not getting up again, no matter what. "Katarina, what am I going to do?"

She laughs. And laughs. Then laughs some more. "You're already doing a good job of looking like an idiot. But you might try pressing the third emerald from the top of the bodice."

I press the first green jewel I see—and my wand makes a bleep! bleep! sound.

"No, that's the wand alarm. I said the third emerald."

I reach for another green jewel.

"NO! You pea brain—that's the Good Night Moonstone!"

"What's that?"

"Never mind. Don't touch it."

I peer down at the front of the dress, which isn't easy when

I'm lying flat on my back on the couch. I reach for the third emerald, and when I press it, there's a low humming sound as the dress inflates all around me. I float to my feet, feeling weightless and graceful.

"*That's* better," I say. I give the girls a little curtsy—and then slowly float up in the air like a balloon that's come untied. Sunny grabs my arm and steadies me.

"How do I stop floating?" I ask Katarina.

"Press the emerald again."

WHOMMMMMP! I plummet back to the couch, facedown this time. This is so annoying!

Katarina flies over and lands on the couch next to me. "Well, copying the dress was an excellent idea. I'm glad I thought of it!"

"Katarina! *Paige* thought of it!" I say.

"Are you saying something, dear? I can't hear you when your face is in a cushion like that."

It's good she can't hear the next thing I say.

Trust me, it's not nice.

CHAPTER

14

Yuck! Just look at all those dead moths on top of Martin's porch light!

The reason I'm looking at them is because I'm hovering outside his front door, with Paige and Sunny on either side holding on to the sleeves of my glittering fairy godmother dress and trying to stop me from floating away.

Katarina, flitting nearby, says, "Bring the *Hindenburg* down!" (I guess that makes me a blimp.) Sunny and Paige finally manage to pull me low enough so my feet reach the porch, and Sunny uses her free hand to ring the doorbell.

Martin answers the door, so dejected that he doesn't even give my dress a second look. "You guys can't be here. I'm grounded."

Paige blocks the door with her foot. "Are your parents home?"

"No, they're both at work. Why?"

I give Martin my brightest smile. "Greetings and salutations,

Martin Shembly!" I say. "I am your fairy godmother. Not every girl . . . uh, boy . . . receives this boon, but you are one of the lucky few. I am here to make your life not-stink."

Martin rolls his eyes. "Good luck with that."

"Really, Martin. I'm your fairy godmother!"

"And I'm the tooth fairy. If I give you a dollar, will you leave me alone?"

Sunny frowns at him. "Martin—Lacey's telling you the truth. All you've got to do is listen to her!"

And then, without asking, Sunny and Paige glide me past him into the house.

"Hold on!" Martin yelps. "I told you, I'm grounded! If my mom finds out you're in here, she'll kill me! And then my dad will kill me again!"

Sunny and Paige park me in the middle of the entryway of the house. It's two stories high—which will work great for what I'm about to do.

"You guys have *got* to get out of here!" Martin says.

Sunny looks nervously up at the ceiling high above us. "Lacey? Are you sure you want to do this?"

"Yes. Absolutely," I say, sounding more certain than I feel. "Let me go."

Sunny and Paige release my sleeves, and I slowly float off the floor, pulled upward by the dress.

Martin's eyes open wide. *"Whoa!"*

As I float up over his head, I'm soooo glad I'm still wearing my jeans. Katarina thought I was being stupid, but it's better to be stupid than to have everyone singing, "I see London, I see France, I see Lacey's Unger-pants." (That happened to me on the jungle gym in second grade, and once was enough.)

Martin excitedly runs up the steps to keep pace with me while I float upward. "This is . . . this is . . . this is . . . incredible! How are you doing that?"

"It's magic! And I'm your fairy godmother!"

"No, really. Tell me! Who needs a jetpack when you've invented a jet *dress*! Please, please, please, tell me how this works! Neodymium magnets? Reverse parachute technology? Nanomotors?" His eyes gleam. "This could be one of the greatest scientific breakthroughs of the twenty-first century!"

"It's not science, it's magic. Magic! Magic! Magic!" I pull out my wand and twirl it in the air. "Who needs neo-whatever magnets when you've got a wand?"

Martin looks a little puzzled, and I think he's starting to believe me. He walks up the stairs as I keep going higher and higher, then finally says, "Can I ask you another question?"

I attempt to sound grand, like Katarina when she's being fancy. "Ask any question your heart desires."

Martin points to the ceiling. "What's going to stop you from hitting *that*?"

I look up—and there's a ginormous fan whirring away a few

feet over my head. Eek! I'm about to be pureed! *"Help!"* I don't sound grand anymore. I sound terrified.

Paige and Sunny start snapping switches on and off, but the fan doesn't slow down even a little.

I reach for the dress-controller emerald but then hesitate—I'm twenty feet in the air, and it would be a long drop to the marble floor beneath me.

"Lacey, watch out!" Paige screams.

At the last possible second, right before the Lacey hits the fan, Martin leaps off the stairway and grabs me around the waist in midair.

And he saves me.

With his extra weight, we glide back down to the floor, safe and sound. Paige and Sunny hold on to my sleeves again, and Martin lets go. He looks at me, wide-eyed and totally shocked.

Finally! He believes I'm a fairy godmother!

Martin makes a pleady face. "Please tell me! I won't say a word to anyone until after you patent it. It's nanomotors, isn't it? Lots and lots of nanomotors. Where are they?" He starts pulling at the cloth of my dress.

I swat at his hands. "Stop that!"

"I have to know how this works! It's driving me crazy."

Suddenly, Katarina buzzes in and hovers an inch away from Martin's nose. "She told you, you ignoramus! I don't know why

this has to be so hard! Lacey Unger-Ware is your fairy god-mother. Deal with it!"

Martin looks at her, and then he sits down on the steps like the wind has been completely knocked out of him.

"*Now* do you believe me?" I ask. I point to Katarina. "Martin, meet my teacher. Katarina, meet Martin."

Martin says, in a low voice that almost sounds like he's talk-ing to himself, "On the one hand, I believe in science and I know that science says fairy godmothers are imaginary. On the other hand, I've read all the Narnia books, all the Harry Potter books, and all the Lord of the Rings books. I know everything in those books is imaginary . . . but it would be so amazing if it was real."

He reaches out gently to touch Katarina's fluttering wings—and she bites him.

"Ow!" Martin says. "Well, you sure seem real."

"She is," Sunny says. Paige and I nod in agreement.

Martin studies Katarina. "How about trolls? Are they real?"

"Yes."

"Leprechauns?"

"Yes."

"Centaurs?"

"Extinct."

"Aww. Elves?"

"Real."

"How *maar*! What about Superman?"

"That's a comic book! Stop asking me these stupid questions! All you need to know is that Lacey's your fairy godmother, and she has between now and the full moon to make your life not-stink."

Martin whistles.

"Does that mean you believe I'm a fairy godmother?" I ask.

"I guess."

Katarina flies over and pokes Martin—hard—with her wand. He says, "Yes, yes! I believe you're a fairy godmother!"

I breathe a sigh of relief. I've made it through step one: he believes me! "There's a lot to talk about," I tell him. "But can we go someplace without a ceiling fan? A chopped-up fairy godmother won't do you any good at all."

CHAPTER 15

Martin leads us down his basement stairs. "This is my work-room. It's kind of messy."

The low-ceilinged space has a tool-covered workbench against one wall, and there's a cluttered plywood table in the middle of the room. The girls glide me over to a beat-up recliner in the corner and I press the controller emerald and thump into the chair, my dress heavy again. "That's better," I say.

Katarina flutters above the table, looking for a place to land. It's not easy, since there's so much bizarre-looking junk: wires and batteries and half-open computers. Katarina finally sits on a volleyball that's wedged between two motors—which both turn on. Then a metal arm raises a tube of toothpaste and squirts her in the face. Katarina screams and tumbles over just before a second metal arm scrubs the volleyball with a toothbrush. "What is this torture device?" she shrieks.

Martin runs over and turns off the motors. "It's not a torture device. It's a machine that brushes your teeth before you get out of bed in the morning. Pretty cool, huh?"

It *is* cool. Martin is probably the smartest kid I've ever met.

But Katarina's not impressed. She furiously raises her wand. I'm a little worried that she's going to turn Martin into a rat or a toad or a cheese sandwich or something. Luckily, she decides to use the wand to clean herself up instead.

Martin sits on a stool, polishes his glasses, and asks, "What's the plan?" He looks at me expectantly, and so do Sunny, Paige, and Katarina.

"Well, my job is to unstink your life, Martin," I explain. "So let's think about *why* your life stinks. It stinks because all the kids hate you. Right? And the kids hate you because you wiped out the water tower, the school carnival, and the club field trips."

Katarina nods. "Plus you're undeniably odd."

"He's not odd—he's interesting!" Sunny says.

"*Right*," Katarina says, completely not meaning it.

Paige says, "Fixing all of those things sounds really hard."

"And expensive!" Martin says. "So, Lacey . . . can you make me a magic cash machine? Or a money tree?"

Katarina shakes her head. "No, she can't. Everyone knows that magic money is funny money!"

"Because it's fake?" I ask.

"No! Because it's funny. It never stops telling jokes."

"Really?"

"Try it."

I pull out my wand and chant, "Don't make me holler; I want a dollar." I toss the spell into the air, and a green dollar bill, surrounded by green sparkles, flutters down to the floor.

Sunny picks it up. "It *looks* real."

Then George Washington's picture on the bill winks at her and says, "I just flew in from the East Coast, and boy, are my arms tired!" George Washington starts laughing like this is the funniest thing he's ever heard. Sunny and Paige roll their eyes.

Katarina glares at him. "That's not funny, Money!"

George laughs on, and on, and on.

Katarina sighs. "He'll laugh until midnight, and then he'll disappear. And *that's* why Lacey can't just conjure up money."

"But what am I going to do with George Washington until then?" I ask.

"Hahahahahahahahahahahahaha," George says.

Katarina zips down, grabs a corner of the dollar bill, and flies it into the little basement bathroom. George yells, "NOOOOOO!" over the sound of flushing.

"And that takes care of that," Katarina says as she flies back into the room. "Please continue the discussion."

We all look at her, shocked. It's not every day you see somebody flush the father of our country down the toilet.

Martin scratches his head. "So, Lacey, if this is going to be about raising money, what are you going to do?"

"Um . . . I just found out you were my client a few hours ago. I'm not really sure—it's going to be hard."

Katarina snorts. "It's not going to be hard. It's going to be impossible!"

Sunny looks desperate. "You've got to be able to do something, Lacey! You're his fairy godmother. Are you sure it's all about the money? To unstink Martin's life, maybe you just need to make the kids at school like him."

"*Im*-possible!" Katarina says.

"It's not *im*-possible!" I say. "Paige went from being a geek at her old school to a popular cheerleader at Lincoln. And that was without any fairy godmother help!"

"Yeah, but my dad got a new job here. It's easier when you move a thousand miles away." Paige turns to Martin. "How do you feel about Alaska?"

"I'm fine with Alaska. I don't think my parents would be."

I grin. "I've got the answer! Nobody has to move to Alaska! Paige needs to use her superpower!"

Paige frowns. "I don't have a superpower."

I nod. "Yes, you do. Your superpower is super popularity. You're just about queen of the school. And when the queen speaks, people listen. Retractable claws and X-ray vision are nothing compared to popularity power."

Sunny nods, too. "Maybe some of Paige's popularity *could* rub off on Martin."

Martin puts his hands together and pretend-begs. "Please, Paige! Please use your power for good!"

Paige gets a deer-in-the-headlights expression. "I don't know if there's anything I can do. I've heard kids talking, and they're really mad."

I tell her, "While I'm thinking of a good magic way to help Martin, it couldn't hurt for you to talk to people, right? Let them know you're on his side."

When Paige hesitates, the hopeful look vanishes from Martin's face. He says, "You're *not* on my side. I don't blame you. I probably wouldn't be either."

"I'm sure I'll think of something magic," I tell Martin. "There are loads of ways to make your life not-stink."

"Name three," Martin says.

"Um . . ." I mumble.

"Name even one!"

"Pop star hair!"

"*What?*" Martin says.

Okay, I admit it: I'm struggling. "What if we're making this too complicated? Maybe all you need is cute hair!" I raise my wand and chant, "You'll have flair, with pop star hair!"

When I toss the spell at Martin's head, his dark hair stands on end like he was just zapped by lightning. Then his hair

flutters back down, and now he's got fluffy bangs and blond highlights and choppy artistic sections sticking up in the back.

He sees his reflection in the basement window and covers his head with his hands. "I. Look. So . . ."

"Pop-starry!" Sunny says.

"Stylish!" Paige says.

"Stupid!" Katarina says. "Not just a little stupid . . . a lot stupid!"

All right. The hair wasn't my best idea.

Martin pulls a hat out of a drawer and covers his head as a gloomy silence fills the room.

Then we all hear a clicking sound from the worktable. It's Katarina, who's knitting something with tiny needles and a tiny pink ball of yarn. This is a strange time to start a new hobby.

"What are you doing, Katarina?" Sunny asks.

"Making a sweater. The nights are cold in Antarctica. So are the days."

Everyone looks at her questioningly, and then they look at me. I say, as if it's not really a big deal, "If Martin doesn't get his dream, Katarina and I will be sent to the South Pole."

Sunny says, "Like for a time-out?"

"Like forever!" I say.

Paige's eyes open wide. "That's harsh!"

"Of course it's harsh," Katarina says. "Haven't you ever read Grimm?"

"The fairy tales?" Martin asks.

"No, the historical documents. People think Grimm is just fun and games, but there are terrible punishments all over the place. Dancing in hot iron shoes. Eyes pecked out by birds. Compared to that, the South Pole is getting off easy. BUT I STILL DON'T WANT TO GO THERE!"

Paige looks at me with sudden determination. "I can't let that happen. I'll use my popularity to help Martin. Maybe it'll be easier than I think."

There's a gurgly "hahaha" from the toilet. Katarina zips into the bathroom and flushes again. Twice.

CHAPTER 16

All my life, I've been kind of a clumsy person. I trip, I hit my elbows on things, and I've broken more dishes at the Hungry Moose than I can count. But right now, gliding down the sidewalk toward home in my dress, I'm *graceful*. As Paige and Sunny hold on to my sleeves to guide me along, I raise my arms like the dancer in Madison's jewelry box and pretend I'm starring in a ballet.

Katarina, flitting nearby, pokes me with her wand. "Stop that. You look like deranged."

I lower my arms, not feeling so graceful anymore. Probably to make me feel better, Sunny says, "I think talking to Martin went pretty well."

Katarina chortles. "Except for that part when Lacey almost got her head chopped off by the fan. Did I ever tell you about that time in Paris with the rusty guillotine? It was *très horrible!* The first thing you need to know about decapitation is—"

"*Don't!*" I say. "Let's just enjoy the beautiful afternoon." I raise my arms again, ballerina style. A girl could get used to traveling like this. It's so . . . elegant!

We reach the intersection, and a breeze hits us as we cross the street. Sunny's hair blows into her face, so she drops my sleeve—for just a second—to brush it away.

Whoosh!

A gust of wind sweeps through the crosswalk, and Paige can't hold on to me by herself. I'm ripped out of her hands. Then I somersault head over heels down the sidewalk like a sparkly tumbleweed. "Oof! Ow! Oof! Geez!" I'm totally out of control.

"Lacey! Come back! Come back!" the girls shout after me. But their voices grow fainter as I roll away.

"Ow! Oof!" I fumble for the right jewel on the dress, trying to make it stop floating. I reach for the emerald, but it's really hard to find since I'm tumbling like a sock in a dryer. By mistake, I press a ruby. *This* makes confetti pelt down on me from the sky.

Where's that stupid emerald? I grab for it again and accidentally hit a sapphire. Sappy romantic music starts to play, like something on the soundtrack of the gushiest princess movie ever. There's gotta be a thousand violins all going at once.

Every single jewel on this ridiculous dress must do something different, so I reach for the emerald one last time—

Then, *WHAM!* I knock into the back of a person walking on the sidewalk. We both fall to the ground. The jolt must have reset everything, because my gown suddenly weighs a ton again, and the music and confetti have stopped.

Feeling woozy from all the rolling, I turn my head—and look straight into the angry eyes of Makayla.

Oh, *geez.*

"Makayla! What are you doing here?" I ask, trying to sound casual.

She points at the nearest house. "I live here. What are *you* doing here?"

I still try to play it cool: "Uh, nothing."

Makayla stands up, rubbing her scraped knees. I wish *I* could stand up, but the dress is too heavy. She peers at my gown. "Why are you wearing that?"

I rummage through my brain, searching for anything to say but the truth. "I was playing dress-up with Sunny," I blurt out Yikes. I've come up with some stupid excuses before, but this is Hall of Fame stupidest.

Makayla looks at me in total disbelief.

"You still play dress-up? What are you, five?" She whips out her cell phone. "I need a picture of this for my blog! You're going to be a permanent fashion-don't. I'm going to call the section 'Lacey What-Not-to-Ware.'"

Wow, my stupid excuse worked, which is good. But a picture

of me in this dress showing up online would be bad. Mom and Dad would wonder where it came from, plus I don't *want* to be a permanent fashion-don't! It would be too humiliating. I twist and turn, trying to sit up, but in my heavy dress I'm like a turtle on its back.

"Stop moving! The picture will be blurry!" Makayla says.

I squirm even harder. "Don't take a picture!"

To keep me still, Makayla puts a foot in the middle of my chest—and one of the jewels on the gown starts flashing brilliant green. "What's that?" Makayla asks, blinking in the light.

As she watches the light, her eyelids get heavier and heavier. "So pretty," she says in a sleepy little voice. She gives a big yawn, curls up on the lawn, and falls fast asleep.

This is bonkers.

Katarina flies up to me and sees the flashing light. "For the love of glitter! Turn off the Good Night Moonstone before you knock out the entire neighborhood."

A second later, a sparrow falls out of the sky onto the lawn, sound asleep, too.

"Turn it off NOW!" Katarina says.

I push the jewel and the flashing stops. "A Good Night Moonstone? Why would you put that on a dress?" I ask.

"In case one's client has to babysit little brothers and sisters, of course. I told you not to touch anything!"

"I didn't! Makayla stepped on me! Why didn't *I* fall asleep?"

"Fairy godmothers are immune."

Sunny and Paige run up, breathless from chasing me down the street. They stare at Makayla.

"Why is she asleep?" Sunny asks.

"I'll tell you later! Help me move her. Be really careful!"

Clunk! Clunk! Clunk!

Makayla's head bonks on every step as we drag her onto her back porch. We try to be careful, but a person is really heavy when you're carrying her around. And it's Sunny and Paige who are doing the work; I'm just floating and hanging on.

The girls flop Makayla into the porch swing as Katarina hovers nearby.

"How long will she sleep?" I ask.

Katarina says, "Don't you remember 'Sleeping Beauty'? A hundred years, of course."

"That's AWFUL!" I shout.

"Don't be so gullible. For every flash of the Good Night Moonstone, Makayla will sleep a minute."

Makayla stretches on the swing and covers her eyes. "Let me sleep just a little more, Mom! I'll get up soon!"

Katarina's wings shift into high gear. "I suggest we get out of here, *now.*"

CHAPTER 17

Katarina zips back in from the bathroom, ready for bed with her hair in little pink curlers and her face covered with shiny cold cream. (It's just like having my aunt Ginny as a roommate.) She sees me turning on my computer. "What are you doing?"

"I want to see if Makayla posted about me on her blog."

"A blog? Is that where ogres live?"

"That's a bog. A blog is where you talk about things that happen to you."

Katarina peers at my computer screen as it boots up. "Who's she talking to?"

"You know . . . the Internet. Anybody who clicks on it."

"And what's she talking about?"

I shrug. "School gossip, mostly. Yesterday she talked about Martin. She thinks she's a big reporter. I want to make sure she doesn't post any pictures of me in the dress."

"She took pictures of you in the dress?" She flies up and starts poking me on the nose with her wand. "This is horrible! Horrible! Horrible!"

"Stop that!" I swat her away. "It's not that big a deal!"

"No, it's not a big deal—it's a catastrophic deal! Fairy godmothers have existed freely for thousands of years because most people think we're imaginary. If the truth comes out, we're done for!"

"Why?"

"People would be hunting us, trapping us, and studying us. That's what happened to dragons."

"Reporters found dragons?"

"No, people found dragons! And now there aren't any more! There have been close calls with fairy godmothers over the years, but we've always managed to hush things up. Leonardo da Vinci even painted a portrait of his fairy godmother—that simp Mona Lisa Vermicelli. Thankfully, we finally talked him into painting out her wings and painting in a smile. The Godmothers' League punished Mona Lisa Vermicelli by turning her into a dung beetle fairy."

"She's a fairy who's a dung beetle?"

"No, worse. She's a fairy godmother *for* dung beetles. And dung beetles only have one dream. Think about it."

I shudder.

The computer finally finishes booting up (it's a hand-me-down from the restaurant, and it's slooooow), and I nervously click on Makayla's link. I sure don't want to be a dung beetle fairy.

Eek. There's a new blog post.

Makayla faces the camera, "Fellow students! This is Makayla Brandice, your eyes and ears on the school. Tonight I want to report about what I saw outside my house this afternoon. Or, rather, who. Lacey Unger-Ware."

Double eek!

Katarina clutches my arm so hard that I yelp.

On the computer screen, Makayla pauses dramatically and I brace for the worst. Then she says, "You're not going to believe this, but Lacey Unger-Ware . . . still plays dress-up!" She smiles a big, fake, smile. "Isn't that sweet! Some of us are growing up too fast, but Lacey is still a child at heart! I was so very charmed that I took a picture for you all to see. . . ."

Katarina grabs my arm again, even harder. "Dung beetles, here we come!"

Then Makayla frowns. "Unfortunately, the picture didn't turn out. But believe me, Lacey looked cute! Cute! CUTE! When you see her tomorrow, pat her on the head and tell her she's all gwowed up now!" She uses an annoying fake little-girl voice that makes me rush to mute the sound.

Katarina sighs with relief. "Well, you look like an unmitigated idiot, but we're safe for now." Then she snickers, flies up, and pats me on the head. "Wacey! You *are* all gwowed up now! Say hewwo to your wittle fwiends at school tomowwow."

Where's *her* mute switch? "Nobody's going to do that."

CHAPTER

18

They *all* do it.

"Hewwo, Wacey!"

"Wacey's all gwowed up now!"

And even "How's wittle Wacey-poo?"

Every kid in school has seen Makayla's video, and probably a hundred people come up to me and pat my head. Katarina, who came with me today in my pocket, snickers every time. Every. Single. Time. You'd think she'd get tired of this joke, but she never does.

On my way to the cafeteria, I walk past Principal Conehurt. At least I'll be safe next to him. "Hi, Lacey!" he says. Then he pats me on the head. "Have a gweat wunch!"

In my pocket, Katarina laughs so loud that I have to cough to cover up the sound. Martin's life may be bad, but mine's pretty stinky too.

OMG! *Martin!* With all the head patting going on, I almost forgot that today's the day that Paige is going to use her popularity powers to help him.

I join Sunny in the cafeteria line, and we both get our glob of mystery lunch. The gunk on our plates might be spaghetti and meatballs; but then again, it might not.

Except for me and Sunny, everyone in the room is glaring at Martin, who's in the corner mopping up more "accidentally" spilled drinks. And I mean everyone. Between the water tower, carnival, and field trips, he did something to upset the whole student body.

Sunny and I pay for our lunches and walk over to the table nearest Martin. As we sit down, the air seems heavy, as if there's a storm coming. But then the cafeteria doors open, letting in a ray of blond sunshine. It's Paige, looking perfect as always. Every head in the room swivels away from Martin and looks at her. Like Sunny said, popularity is her superpower.

Paige walks to the drink machine, fills a large cup of lemonade, and approaches Martin, holding the too-full drink carefully in front her. There are snickers from the room, and expectation builds with every step Paige takes. Makayla yells across the room, "Don't drop your drink, Paige! That would be *terrible!*"

Taylor laughs. "Good one, Makayla!"

When Paige stops right in front of Martin with the drink, everyone in the cafeteria holds his or her breath.

"Here, Martin! I thought you might be thirsty," Paige says. And then . . . she hands him the cup.

The other kids gasp and look confused. *She's being nice to him?* This wasn't the splashy, humiliating end that everyone was expecting.

Paige stands next to Martin and looks at the crowd. "Okay, everybody, I want to talk to you. Enough is enough! Martin didn't mess things up on purpose. So let's stop being mean to him, right now."

Martin looks up at the crowd, daring to hope. Paige sounds so sure of herself, and she's so self-confident, that it really seems like this could work. Without taking her eyes off the other kids, Paige puts her hand on Martin's shoulder. "Who's with me?"

There's a moment of silence. If we're lucky, it will be a Lincoln Middle School miracle and everyone will cheer and there will be a lot of hugging.

Instead . . .

. . . somebody throws a meatball right at Paige's face. It bounces off her forehead and rolls down the cafeteria floor. Paige wipes off some tomato sauce and looks down at her hand, shocked.

"That's not funny!" she says.

A moment later, there's a hailstorm of food flying at Paige— and at Sunny, Martin, and me, too.

There's spaghetti and Jell-O and salad greens. There's bread

and carrots and half-eaten brownies. There's yogurt and string cheese and juice boxes. I could go on, but I'm pretty sure that by now you've got the idea.

Lincoln is a pretty relaxed school, but there are still loads of different groups that don't like each other. On a normal day, the French Club squabbles with the Spanish Club. The football players fight with the marching band about field practice time. Even Scott's unicyclists compete with the skateboarders for side-walk space.

But at this moment, Martin has achieved the impossible. The school is totally united in one common goal: to throw as much food at the four of us as possible. You'd think there'd be *somebody* who'd be on Martin's side, and maybe there even is. But throwing spaghetti is just too much fun.

One of the PE teachers, Mrs. Brinker, runs in from the hall-way blowing her whistle. It takes the kids a while to stop tossing food (once you've got a handful of green beans, it's hard *not* to throw them), but finally there's only the sound of goo dripping off the walls—and off me, Paige, Sunny, and Martin.

Mrs. Brinker lets her whistle drop on its cord, her face angry and red. She points at us. "You four! Go get cleaned up!"

Then she looks at the rest of the kids in the cafeteria. "Every-body else . . . you've got cleanup detention for the next week! And this afternoon, the first thing you get to do is clean up this cafeteria. If I come back and see one speck of food on the walls, you're going to clean it again on Saturday."

Makayla stands up and says, in her syrupy-sweet voice, "But Mrs. Brinker! I didn't have anything to do with it. I'm just here reporting this for my blog."

Mrs. Brinker sneers. "Is that a fact, Makayla? Then why do I see green Jell-O in your hands?"

Then Mrs. Brinker points at Paige, Sunny, Martin, and me again. "I said out!"

I thought the kids hated Martin before, but as we slink out, the looks they give us are burning hot. If the food that's stuck to us burst into flames, I wouldn't be all that surprised.

Sunny, Paige, and I take showers in the girls' locker room. Every time I think I'm finally clean, I find a little more food—and believe me, tapioca in your ears is *gross*.

Sunny and I dry off and change into our gym clothes, but Paige stays in her stall, the water going full blast.

Sunny tells me, "When you see food fights in movies, they look like a lot of fun. But that hurt!" She rubs her cheek, which is still red from where an orange hit her. I feel awful; it almost looks like she got slapped in the face.

I hear a little squeak from my food-covered sweater. I pick it up and scrape a big wad of applesauce off the pocket. Katarina squirms out, gasping. "Those children are criminals!" she wails. "I don't know what this 'cleanup detention' is, but I sincerely hope there's a firing squad involved!"

When Paige finally comes out of the shower, her eyes are red from crying.

"Are you all right?" I ask.

"No, I'm not all right," she says. "Martin's life still stinks, and now mine does, too."

Sunny tries to make a joke out of it. "Your life doesn't stink. It's just covered in spaghetti sauce."

Paige doesn't laugh. "It's not funny! That was the most humiliating thing to ever happen to me!" She pulls on her gym clothes as fast as she can.

This day is getting worse and worse. "I'm so sorry. I never, ever thought that would happen. And I never should have asked you to put your popularity on the line."

Paige gives me an icy look. "No, you shouldn't have. You used me, Lacey. It wasn't my job to fix Martin's problems, it was your job. Starting right now, I'm out of the godmother posse."

Paige storms out of the locker room.

I'm too shocked to follow her. This is one of the worst days of my life.

I manage to reach a toilet stall and close the door before I start to cry.

CHAPTER 19

As Martin and I sit on the curb waiting for our parents to pick us up, Katarina sticks her head out of my backpack. She tells Martin in a surprisingly kind voice, "The fairy godmothers have a saying that I'd like to share with you right now."

Martin looks a little hopeful. "Okay."

"You're DOOMED!"

"Shut up, Katarina! You're not helping!"

Principal Conehurst wasn't much help, either. All he did was send Sunny, Paige, Martin, and me home. Since Paige (who didn't say one word to me) and Sunny have already gone, now it's just me here on the curb with a very sad-looking Martin.

Very, *very* sad. No wonder—his life is wrecked and his fairy godmother hasn't come up with a single magic thing that will help him. I wish the Godmothers' League believed in teachers who actually told you what to do.

When I feel sad, Sunny always gets me a cookie to make me feel better, and I wish I had a cookie to give Martin right now. It wouldn't fix his life, but at least it would cheer him up a little. Hey! I *could* get him one!

I pull out my wand and chant, "A big cookie would, make you feel good." And then I toss the spell at Martin.

There is a whistling sound from overhead . . .

. . . and *WHAMMO!* A four-foot-wide cookie drops from the sky and whacks Martin on the head. He falls to the curb, the shattered pieces of the big cookie all around him.

"Martin! Are you okay?"

He sits up, rubbing his head. "Why did you just drop a giant cookie on me? That's just plain *strange!*"

"I thought a cookie would make you feel better."

"Well, it hurt! And I don't need any more food thrown at me today."

"I'm really, really sorry, and the cookie was a mistake. But we're just getting started! Sometimes it's a little rocky in the beginning. Don't worry—I'm not going to give up."

From deep in the bottom of my backpack comes a muffled "Martin, you're DOOMED!"

He ignores Katarina and looks at me with a sad expression. "Lacey, this isn't working. It's not you—it's me. I don't want to do this anymore."

Wait—this sounds just like the kind of things guys say in

those romantic movies my mom loves. "Are you breaking up with me?" I say. "I'm your fairy godmother! You can't!"

"Yes, I can. It's hopeless. I've always been the weird kid, and I know it. I'm smart, and I wear glasses, and I'm interested in stuff that nobody else likes. My dad says my life will get better in college, after being horrible in middle school and even worse in high school."

His dad doesn't believe in sugarcoating things, does he?

"Right now a fairy godmother's not going to help me much, unless you can put me in a time machine and make me a freshman at Cal Tech."

"But it doesn't have to be horrible for you! I can help!"

"Nerds don't get fairy godmothers. Wedgies, yes. Fairy godmothers, no."

"We just have to keep trying!"

"Look, Lacey. You can't raise the money to fix what I did, and you can't make the kids stop hating me. Go help some girl find a pretty dress like fairy godmothers are supposed to do and leave me alone."

A car pulls up, and there's an impatient beep from its horn. Martin gets in, and the car drives away.

Katarina reaches out from my backpack, grabs a chunk of giant cookie, and munches on it. "Well, that's the way the cookie crumbles," she says. "Antarctica, here we come."

"We've got loads of time!"

"Think about what he just said, Lacey. You got fired. Canned. Made redundant. Kicked to the curb. Oh look—we're already *on* the curb. How very, very convenient."

"I'll go talk to him."

She tosses a chunk of cookie at me and shouts, "And tell him what? *You don't have a plan!*"

And she's right. I don't.

Mom takes me home to get a change of clothes, and then I spend the afternoon at the Hungry Moose, feeling miserable. (Katarina has had enough of pockets and backpacks, so she's staying home.) At least it's quiet here in the restaurant dining room—we're closed for a couple of hours between lunch and dinner, and Mom has walked Madison down the street to her ballet class.

What am I going to do about Martin? There's got to be something. I just can't think of it. My magic wand is in my pocket, practically begging me to use it.

Except Katarina's right. I need a plan. There are so many things I can't do. I can't make money. I can't do spells that last past midnight. I can't do something so big that people will figure out it's magic. I can't get godmother help from Katarina. I can't get human help from Paige. I can't even make Martin feel better with a cookie.

It's all can't, can't, can't. I need a *can*!

There's gotta be *something* I can do! Is there a way I can change Martin for just one day that will make him popular? What if he saves puppies from a burning building? (Too dangerous.) Wins the Guinness World Record for Loudest Burp? (Too gross.) Becomes the world's best tap dancer? (Too tappy.) What about turning him into a tapping, burping puppy rescuer? (Even thinking about this makes my head hurt.)

Dad takes a break from toasting garlic bread and sits down next to me. "Principal Conehurst said that you and the girls were sticking up for a boy who was getting picked on. I'm proud of you."

"It was Paige, mostly."

"Ask her to come by with her dad and I'll treat them to dinner."

That would mean that she was still my friend, and that she was talking to me. Neither of those things is true. So I just say, "Okay."

Dad says, "It's really hard to stick up for the kid everyone thinks is a loser. But nobody's a loser, really, and you're smart enough to see that."

What Dad doesn't know is that I'm not smart about anything.

Just then, the latch on the locked door rattles. "We're closed until five!" Dad shouts without getting up.

There's a tapping on the window near the door, and a round-faced old man wearing a green cowboy hat peers in at us.

I instantly know who it is, but Dad looks confused. "Why does that guy look so familiar?" he whispers to me.

"It's the Abner's Pickles guy," I say. I know this partly because he's on a zillion jars of pickles, and partly because I did a magic spell once that helped a girl from Lincoln Middle School get a part in one of Abner's TV commercials. But that doesn't mean I'm not amazed to see Abner himself tapping on the window of the Hungry Moose. What's he doing here?

Dad unlocks the door and Abner strides in, his shiny green cowboy boots clicking on the tile.

"Hi there," Abner says. Even though he's got a big, toothy smile, he also looks a little tired. "I was driving past and saw your sign. 'The Hungry Moose.' This is my kind of place."

"Dinner's at five," Dad says. "You should come back."

"Can I get some takeout? To be honest, I need a little comfort food. I just spent a week in focus groups for a new product, and it crashed and burned. I thought people would love pickle-flavored ice cream, but even pregnant ladies hated it. A year's worth of research and development down the drain."

It's too bad he wasted all that work, but even I could have told him that pickle-flavored ice cream was a bad idea.

Abner looks so sad that Dad hands him a menu. "Here at the Hungry Moose, we *specialize* in comfort food. I'll make up anything you want."

"Thank you so much," Abner says. He makes a lot of *mmmm* sounds as he looks through the menu.

Dad asks, "What brings you to town?"

"I just built a little vacation cabin near the lake." Abner puts down the menu. "If it's not too much trouble, I'd like one of everything."

"I'd be happy to . . . on one condition."

Abner looks at him suspiciously. "What is it?"

Dad disappears into the kitchen and comes back with a five-gallon tub of Abner's Pickles. "Will you autograph this for me?"

Abner laughs. "Not a problem!"

Dad waves at me. "Lacey! You've got to get a picture of this!"

I use my phone to take a picture of Abner signing the jar and Dad making a goofy face and pointing. I'm sure this will get framed and put on the Hungry Moose wall next to the photo of the egg with three yolks.

Then Dad stands me next to Abner to take a picture of us together, too. "Lacey, smile!" If Abner can smile after failing with pickle ice cream, I should be able to smile after failing as a fairy godmother.

But somehow, I just can't.

CHAPTER 20

"The pickle guy showed up again? Was it another one of your misbegotten spells?" Katarina asks me as the waves lap against her boat. (Tonight, her 60 percent of the bedroom looks like an endless, calm, blue ocean.)

"No, he saw the restaurant sign. He was driving by on his way to the lake."

Katarina peers at the picture of Dad and Abner on my phone. "Your father is easily impressed. Just look at him. And that Abner. Pickles! What a way to waste your life."

"Abner's Pickles are Sunny's favorite. And he gives a lot of money to charity."

I tap the picture to enlarge the part of the label that reads *A percentage of every sale goes to fund good causes in your community.*

"Well, hooray for Abner. I don't know why you're wasting time taking pictures of pickles when you should be thinking about Martin."

Katarina's right. Abner's Pickles has absolutely nothing to do with my problem. I'm about to put down my phone when I read the "good causes" part on the label again. I say, "Wait a minute! Lincoln Middle School is a good cause."

"I suppose."

"And our school is in our community!"

"So what?"

"Maybe he could sponsor a new carnival. Or fix the water tower. It could have a sign on it that says 'This water tower brought to you by Abner's Pickles.'"

"You're delusional."

"No, I'm completely lusional!" (Is that a word?) "Tomorrow I'm going to go talk to Abner and ask him to help Lincoln Middle School."

Katarina looks at me thoughtfully as she bobs up and down in her little boat. "You're forgetting something."

"What?"

"It's Martin you're supposed to be focusing on here—he's got to be involved, too. Cinderella's fairy godmother didn't go to the ball for Cinderella; she made it possible for Cinderella to go to the ball. For Martin's life to not-stink, he's the one who needs to get the credit."

Suddenly curious, I ask, "Did you actually know Cinderella's fairy godmother?"

Katarina makes a retching sound deep in her throat.

"You didn't like her?" I ask.

"No. Cinderella's godmother was lovely. I'm seasick." Katarina, looking woozy, clutches the edge of her boat as it bobs up and down on the waves.

Suddenly, a cold breeze gusts out of Augustina's magic portal, which is now a couple of inches wide. I tell Katarina, "It's getting bigger!"

"Don't be silly. Of course it isn't."

Then another, much stronger breeze blasts out of the portal into my room, and a thin sheet of ice forms on top of the waves. A moment later, the sky behind Katarina turns from deep blue to steel gray.

The ice thickens, and Katarina's little boat stops bobbing and freezes in place.

Katarina stares at the frozen sea around her, worried. Finally, she nods. "The portal *is* getting bigger. The fairies are sending us a preview of coming attractions."

"What do you mean?"

"If you don't help Martin, this is what our future will look like. Ice, cold, and Antarctica. And that's not the bee's knees, as you kids say."

That's not something even my *grandparents* say, but I still shiver, and not just from the cold.

CHAPTER 21

Ka-scrape, ka-scrape, ka-scrape is the sound I hear when I wake up the next morning.

I open my eyes and see that the portal got even bigger overnight. Not a lot bigger, but enough so now there's not only wind blowing into the room, there's snow, too. The *ka-scrape* noise is from a little snow shovel that scoops up the snow on the floor and dumps it back through the portal.

Katarina is perched on the edge of my dresser, taking the curlers out of her hair.

"What's going on?" I ask sleepily.

"Snow removal, obviously."

Then there's a terrified little screech from the snow shovel, and it gets sucked right through the portal. Katarina, who doesn't look away from the mirror, flicks her wand to create another shovel. "Augustina is trying to make my life difficult with her portal spell. I'm not letting that blue-haired buzzard get the best of me! Watch an expert at work."

"I can't! I have my internship at the petting zoo this morning."

"Leave! I'll stay here and look after things. And you, missy, figure out how you're going to get Martin to go with you to talk to Abner."

"How am I going to do that?" I ask Gus the pony at the petting zoo. Gus ignores me and keeps eating his oats.

For the next two hours, I try to figure things out. And I come up with—*nothing.* It's really hard to be a fairy godmother to someone who doesn't want to be fairy godmothered.

Even if I do talk Martin into going, how will we get to Abner's house? The lake is pretty far. When Dad drives us up to swim in the summer, it takes ninety-one bottles of beer on the wall to get there; over two hundred bottles if the traffic is bad.

As I'm doing all this thinking, I look out the petting zoo gate and see Scott, his face shiny with sweat, slowly pedaling up the steep hill on his unicycle.

"Hi, Scott!" I call.

He's so breathless, he has trouble getting the words out. "Hi, Lacey! Did you forget that the Uni-Cylones were practicing hills today?" (Only when he says it, there are a lot of spaces from panting between the words. I mean, a *lot*.)

Eight more breathless unicyclists pedal up the hill behind him. I *did* forget about the club. Maybe, since I have no Martin ideas, I can hang out with them for a little while.

"I'm almost finished here," I tell Scott. "I'll meet you guys at the top of the hill."

"Did you bring your unicycle?" he asks.

"Uh . . . of course!" I lie. Not only did I not bring my unicycle, I never even asked Mom and Dad about getting one. (I've had a lot on my mind lately.)

The second Scott and the other unicyclists are gone, I pull my wand out of my pocket. What can I zap? Then I notice a Frisbee that some kid tossed onto the roof of the feed shed. That's perfect. It's even round like a wheel.

I raise the wand and chant, "Frisbee, Frisbee, on the shed, be a unicycle instead!" When I toss the spell, a swirl of sparkles forms over the Frisbee, and it transforms into a gleaming silver unicycle with a bright pink seat.

The unicycle tilts upright, rolls off the shed roof, and lands at my feet. *Very* cool. But when I grab for it, it rolls out of reach. "Come back here," I tell it.

Instead, *whoosh*, it flies to the other side of the fence. It's not acting like a unicycle—it's acting like a Frisbee. "Stop flying! You're not a Frisbee anymore! You're a unicycle!"

It ignores me and zooms up and over the treetops in a shiny silver blur, out of sight. "Come back! Come back! Come back!" I call.

But the Frisbee-unicycle doesn't return. I peer over the tops of the trees, looking for any sign of it. It's gone! I'd need something like Martin's jetpack to catch it, if the jetpack really worked instead of just making farting noises.

Then I have a lightbulb moment, as if there's a giant idea light right over my head.

And the bulb keeps blinking one word: *Jetpacks. Jetpacks. Jetpacks.*

I send two quick texts, one to Scott to tell him I can't do the Uni-Cyclones today because I'm going to have to help at the Hungry Moose (not true), and one to Mom to tell her I'm going to be working on a project with Martin this afternoon (completely true). Then I race out of the petting zoo.

CHAPTER 22

I skulk around the side of Martin's house like a burglar and peer down into the basement window, but the room is dark. Then, above me, I hear the sound of a violin playing a slow, sad classical piece. It's coming from one of the second floor windows.

I've got to be a little sneaky—there are two cars in the driveway, so Martin's parents must be home. I cup my hands around my mouth and call, "Psssst! Hey, Martin! Martin!" And then I add about a million more *pssssts* in.

Finally, the violin stops playing. Martin opens the window and sticks his head out. "Lacey, are you crazy? What are you doing here?"

"I want to show you something."

"Go away! I'm grounded, remember? And I'm supposed to be practicing!"

"Take a little break. It'll be worth it." I raise my wand over my head and chant, "You won't believe your eyes, when my back-pack flies!" and toss the spell over my shoulder.

Two jets of brilliant pink sparkles burst out from behind me, and I shoot up into air above the trees like I'm tied to a rocket.

I grab the front straps to hold on, and suddenly I slow down and hover, with Martin's house far below me. That was scary! But so far, so good.

I pull on the left strap, and I glide left. I pull on the right strap, and I glide right. I pull down, and with the backpack still spewing pink sparkles, I glide down until I'm face-to-face with Martin outside his window. His eyes are just about popping out of his head.

"Welcome to the Future Flyers Club," I tell him. "Today's meeting is all about jetpacks."

"*Awesome!*" Martin says. "Except . . ."

"Except what?"

"Do the sparkles really need to be so . . . pink?"

He's right. Jetpacks are usually such a boy thing: high-tech and sci-fi. But when you add a ton of pink sparkles, they turn into something that my sister, Madison, might have dreamed up. "Sorry. Fairy godmothering is all about pink sparkles. So does that mean you don't want one?"

"Are you kidding? Of course I want one. I don't care if you paint *me* pink! Make me one! Make me one now!"

I grab onto the window frame and climb into the room.

Within seconds, Martin's entire room is filled with pink rocket exhaust.

"You've got to turn off the jetpack," Martin says.

He's right—but how? It's not like I can just *ask* the jetpack to turn itself off. Or can I? "Jetpack? Please turn off."

Problem solved. It looks like an ordinary backpack again.

Sometimes I just love magic.

"We're going on a field trip," I tell Martin. "I need your backpack, too."

Right then there's a voice from outside the room: it's Martin's mom. "I don't hear any practicing in there."

Martin picks up his violin and bow and starts playing again. He whispers, "I can't go anyplace. I've got to practice for another two hours."

"Two hours! That's a lot of practicing."

"My mom wants me to audition for this fancy teacher in Chicago. He only takes three students a year, and she thinks I need to be one of them. So I'm stuck here."

I give him a smug smile. "Lucky for you, you've got a fairy godmother." I raise my wand and chant, "Pick up the slack, till Martin gets back." Then I toss the spell at the violin and the bow. They leap out of Martin's hands and, floating in the air, start playing all by themselves.

Sometimes I even impress myself.

CHAPTER

23

With the magic jetpacks scattering sparkles behind us, we fly high above the streets. I glide along like a normal person—or at least as normal as you can be when you're wearing a magic jetpack—and Martin zips around like a maniac, leaving trails of brilliant pink sparkles in the sky.

I'm worried that people will look up and see us, but nobody does. For one thing, the jetpacks don't make a single sound. And for another, the few people who are on the street are all staring at their phones, not up into the sky. We could be dancing the cha-cha up here and no one would see because they're texting.

Martin zooms half a block ahead of me. "Come back!" I shout. "I need to talk to you."

He ignores me and pulls his backpack straps so he can do crazy loop-the-loops instead. "This is so *maar!*"

Martin soars high above me until he's just a little speck in the clouds, and then he zooms back down until I'm sure he's going to smash on the ground. I shriek and cover my eyes. I wonder what happens to fairy godmothers whose clients end up squashed like bugs?

"This is really, really, really, *really maar!*" he says, sounding very close.

I open my eyes and see Martin right next to me, not squished. "I wish I could fly forever," he says.

He's acting like this is a game, when it's really serious fairy godmother business. "We can't fly around all day," I say. "We have to go talk to Abner at his lake house."

Martin looks at me, confused. "Abner who?"

I explain all about seeing Abner at the Hungry Moose yesterday, and about how I think he might be able to give us money for the school. I finish up by saying, "And *you* have to be the one to ask Abner. You were the one who caused all the problems, so you have to be the one to solve them. Sound like a plan?"

"Sounds like a plan." Martin points up ahead of us. "There's the lake. Which one is his house?"

The lake glitters in the distance, and there are dozens of houses around it, maybe even hundreds. "I'm not really sure," I say. "He said he just built a little cabin. All we have to do is find it."

Martin and I jet around the lake, peering down at the houses. We see big ones and small ones, but we don't see anything that looks like a new cabin. I never thought this would be so hard.

When we've circled almost the entire lake, Martin starts to laugh.

"What's funny?" I ask.

"I think I found his 'little cabin.'" He points down at the biggest house I've ever seen, along with a huge garage and what looks like a barn.

"That's not a cabin!"

"No. But I'm sure it belongs to Abner."

"How do you know?"

"Look at the swimming pool."

I study the oddly-shaped pool. It's not a rectangle—it's a curvy-sided oblong, and its walls are green instead of the usual blue. I start laughing. "It's a pickle?"

Martin nods. "A *big* pickle!"

CHAPTER 24

We skid to a stop on the lawn outside Abner's house, leaving behind two swirly clouds of pink sparkles. A moment later, we just look like two ordinary kids wearing ordinary backpacks.

Martin stares at the big, green front door. "So now we ring the bell and ask Abner for money?"

"I guess." I was so worried about getting here that I didn't really think about what we would say. I take a deep breath and then go to the front door and ring the bell.

A tall, no-nonsense-looking woman wearing a housekeeper's tunic opens the door and stares down at us. "Yes?"

Trying to sound confident, I say, "Hi! We're here to see Abner."

"He's very busy. You can call his office in the city and set up an appointment."

Martin flashes a confident smile. "He's expecting us. We're, uh, writing a report about the history of pickles in America. And you can't write about the current state of condiments without including the Big Pickle himself."

The woman starts to close the door. "As I said, he's very busy. Good luck on your report."

"Mrs. Gibbs, wait," a voice calls out from inside the house. "I have a few minutes to spare." A moment later, Abner appears at the door, smiling. He reaches out to shake our hands. "I'm always happy to talk about pickles! Come in, kids!" He looks at me a little closer. "And hey there—aren't you the Hungry Moose girl?" I nod, and he smiles. "Great to see you again!"

Abner leads us through the gigantic living room, which has a huge stone fireplace and a high beamed ceiling. You could fit my entire house in here.

Then the three of us go into a smaller room that only *half* my house could fit inside. I only have one word to say about it: green. The walls are green. The carpet is green. The ceiling is green. The lights are green. Even the desk is green.

A stained-glass window covers half of one wall. It shows a pickle jar with the words *Veni, Vidi, Condivi* on it.

"I just had the window installed," Abner says proudly.

"What does it say?" Martin asks.

"The story of my life. In Latin, it means, 'I came, I saw, I pickled.'"

Abner points at another wall that has shelves covered with

knickknacks. "I was so poor when I was a kid, I never had anything to play with. Now that I'm grown up, I try to collect every pickle toy that's ever been made."

How many pickle toys can there be? But when I look closer at the shelves, there are dozens. A pickle piggy bank. Pickles with red Santa hats. Pickle flashlights. Stuffed animals—I mean, stuffed pickles. Pickle cars. Pickle Christmas ornaments. It's a peck of pickles.

On the middle shelf, there's a whole miniature carnival, where all the rides—none of them more than a couple of inches high—are shaped like pickles. There's a little Ferris wheel with pickle gondalas. A pickle teacup ride. A pickle merry-go-round. A pickle Tilt-a-Whirl.

"Oooh, look," Martin says. "There's even a roller coaster!"

Abner flicks a switch, and a little pickle bobsled moves up a track and then plunges down. "I named the coaster The Terrifica."

"Because it's so terrific?" I ask.

"No. *Terrifica* is Latin for *terrifying*. A good name for a roller coaster, don't you think?"

Abner motions toward the chairs in front of his huge desk. "Have a seat, kids." We sit down, and Abner walks to a cabinet and opens it. Only it's not a cabinet—it's actually a refrigerator that's filled with jars of pickles. "I have every variety of Abner's Pickle products right here." He pulls out a freezer drawer at the bottom, and cold air drifts up. (Which reminds me of my bedroom.) Abner hands both me and Martin ice-cream bars.

Green ice-cream bars.

"My newest concoction," Abner says. "Try it."

I hesitate. It looks like a pickle. It smells like a pickle.

"EW! YUCK!" Martin blurts. "It tastes like a pickle."

Abner looks crushed. "All my product people told me pickle ice cream was a great idea."

Martin shakes his head. "Sir! One thing I've learned from my own inventions: some ideas are just *bad*." He holds up the green ice-cream bar. "And this is one of them. You need to move on to your *next* idea."

Yikes! If I'd known Martin was going to say that, I would have jabbed him with my elbow. Now it's too late. But maybe Abner will appreciate an honest opinion. . . .

He doesn't. Abner's face slowly turns red, and then he takes the ice-cream bars away from us and throws them in the trash. (I'm sorry he's mad, but I'm also kind of happy I didn't have to eat the pickle ice cream.)

Abner sits down. Before, he was kind of like a friendly grandfather showing off his cool stuff. Now, thanks to Martin, he's got an expression I recognize from Katarina: cranky. "So . . ." he says. "You two are here to write a history of pickles in America."

Abner looks so *un*-friendly that I know Martin and I need to be really careful about what we say next. We'll chat for a while, and then, finally, carefully sneak in our idea that Abner could help our school.

"Actually . . ." Martin says, "we're hoping you can give us some money for Lincoln Middle School. You see, I wrecked the water tower, which ruined the carnival, which canceled the field trips. If you could pay for all that stuff, it would be excellent. Or, as the elves say, *maar!*"

"Well, as *I* say . . . get out of my office! I should have known you were here to talk about money, not pickles." Abner stands up. "I've worked very hard for a very long time. And this is my advice to you children: get out there and work hard, just like I did. No one's going to give you a handout."

"But your jars say you give money to good causes," I tell Abner. "And Lincoln Middle School is a good cause."

He walks over and opens the study door. "My foundation

handles the charitable donations. Mrs. Gibbs will give you the number—the grant process usually takes about a year."

I ask him, "Could they do it faster? Like, by next weekend?"

He shakes his head. "I'm sorry; that's not possible." He calls into the house, "Mrs. Gibbs! Escort these two youngsters out! Mrs. Gibbs!"

And our meeting with Abner is over.

CHAPTER
25

Martin and I jetpack home, neither of us talking much. This time there's no loop-the-looping or happy shouting in Elvish. Even our jetpacks' pink sparkles seem a little less bright and twinkly.

I was so sure that Abner would help us. But it's almost like what happened with Paige—I tried to use Abner, and he got mad. Sure, Martin was the one who blurted out the stuff, but I was the one who should have planned things better. "I'm really sorry, Martin," I say. "I thought talking to Abner would work."

"*Nothing's* going to work. My life is going to stink forever."

"No, it's not! It's like Abner says—we just have to work hard and help ourselves."

"*How?* I can't pay for a new water tower. Or the carnival. Or the field trips."

Blink! Blink! Blink! The idea lightbulb over my head is back on, and I suddenly see exactly what we can do. And it doesn't depend on Paige. It doesn't depend on Abner. It just depends on plain old fairy godmother me. "Martin!" I shout. "We can put on our own carnival! A big one! We'll raise a lot of money and rebuild the water tower and get the field trips back!"

I'm disappointed to see that Martin's not nearly as excited as I am. "My Cub Scout troop held a carnival two years ago. We worked like Romulan salt miners, and we only made forty-three dollars."

"That's because you didn't have this!" I pull out my magic wand. "It'll be a *magic* carnival! The best carnival anybody's ever seen."

Martin thinks about it. "You can do that?"

"I know things haven't worked great so far. But yes, I can do that! We can plan it this week, and hold the carnival on Friday and Saturday. And we'll be making real money, not funny money."

"That might work," Martin says, thinking. Then he breaks into a big smile. "That *will* work!" He's so excited that he does loop-the-loops in his jetpack again. "Yes! We'll put on a magic carnival at the school and make enough money to fix everything!"

"Right! And you can get the credit and be a hero for all the kids so your life won't stink anymore!"

A few minutes later, we're flying over the parking lot at Lincoln, which is empty because it's Saturday.

I zoom down until I'm hovering just above the pavement. "Next weekend, the Ferris wheel can go here."

Martin zips down next to me. "And the Tilt-a-Whirl over there."

"And bumper cars over there!"

"And don't forget a roller coaster," Martin says.

"That can go way in back. There can be games in the middle, over there."

"Like video games?"

"No—carnival games. You know, like the ring toss thing where you spend a lot of money trying to win a little toy."

"You sound like an expert."

"Last summer at the state fair, my dad spent over twenty dollars trying to win Madison a troll doll."

Martin smiles. "Bring on the trolls! But not the real ones, okay?"

"Got it. No real trolls." Then I point to the far end of the parking lot. "I'll do spells to make booths for the food court all along that side. At the fair, everybody ate like crazy."

"How are we going to explain where the carnival came from? We can't tell them it's magic."

"You're the third person I've been a fairy godmother for, and you know what I've learned? People never think it's magic. We'll just say that the stuff was donated for the weekend, and people will believe it. We're good to go!" I'd pat myself on the back if I weren't wearing a jetpack.

There's suddenly a loud, clattering sound right behind us. We both look over and see Makayla, who's holding a metal trash can and staring at us with her mouth hanging open.

What's she doing at school on a Saturday? Makayla's the last person I want to meet when I'm flying with a sparkle-spewing magic jetpack.

"Makayla," I stammer as I float ten feet above her head. "This isn't what it looks like."

Makayla points at us and shrieks: "You have jetpacks!"

Hmm . . . I guess it *is* what it looks like.

Makayla runs toward the outside cafeteria doors, waving her arms over her head. "You guys have to come see this! You're not going to believe it!"

Oh, geez—the kids must be back today cleaning food off the walls.

I shout, "Jetpacks, please turn off!" The sparkles disappear, and Martin and I both drop the remaining couple of feet onto the ground.

A second later, two dozen kids and Mrs. Brinker stream out of the cafeteria, led by Makayla. Makayla points at us and shouts, "Here they are!"

The group stops in front of us, staring. And Martin and I stare right back.

"I thought you said they were flying," Mrs. Brinker asks Makayla.

"They were! They were ten feet off the ground! And there were lots and lots of pink sparkles coming out of their backpacks."

Mrs. Brinker rolls her eyes. "Okay. Everybody back to work!"

"I'm telling the truth," Makayla says. "I saw it!" Makayla tugs first on my backpack and then on Martin's. "Make them fly!" she tells us.

Martin makes the crazy sign by circling his finger near his head. There are snickers from the kids.

"Stop that!" Makayla shrieks. "You *were* flying! And there were sparkles everywhere!"

Mrs. Brinker says, "Makayla, I've heard enough. I mean it. Everybody back to work!"

The kids hesitate, and Mrs. Brinker blows her whistle. "Back to work or you're all going to be here tomorrow, too!"

"But . . . but . . . I saw them! I'm not lying!" Makayla says.

I need to do something before Makayla has a total meltdown. And I *really* need to make sure that no one believes her flying story. So I say, "Makayla, you really saw a lot of sparkles?"

"Yes! All around you and Martin!"

I turn to Mrs. Brinker. "This happened to me once at the

Hungry Moose. It's from the cleaning fumes! She should probably lie down!"

Mrs. Brinker, looking worried, puts her hand on Makayla's forehead. "You *are* clammy."

Blaine Anders clutches his forehead dramatically and says, "Mrs. Brinker! I see pink sparkles, too!"

"That's not funny, Blaine," Mrs. Brinker says, but she still looks worried, not mad. She tells the kids, "That's enough cleaning for the day!"

The kids don't need to be told twice—they scurry away. Makayla looks at me and Martin uncertainly, as if she's starting to doubt what she saw with her own eyes.

Mrs. Brinker puts an arm around her. "Come on, dear. I'll drive you home."

As she leads Makayla away, Martin gives me a high five.

It was pretty clever, if I do say so myself.

CHAPTER
26

Instead of using the jetpacks, Martin and I walk back to his house. We don't need anyone else to see us flying this afternoon.

But four people *do* see us—walking, not flying. It's Scott and the terrible trio: his three bratty little brothers. One of them is riding on his shoulders, and the other two are pulling him along by his sleeves.

"Hi, Lacey," Scott says. "I thought you were working at the restaurant this afternoon."

That's the problem with lying—sometimes you get caught. I tell him, "Uh . . . I had to help Martin with something."

The little boys smirk at their brother, and the one on Scott's shoulders says, in an annoying singsongy voice, "Scott's girlfriend has a new boyfriend!"

The other two boys start repeating, "Scott's girlfriend has a new boyfriend! Scott's girlfriend has a new boyfriend!"

I *told* you they were terrible.

I blush. Scott blushes. Martin blushes.

Scott and Martin both say at the same time: "She's not my girlfriend!"

And I just blush some more while the little boys laugh at us.

Scott tells me, "I have to get the monsters to the park. See you guys later."

After he races away, Martin looks at me. "Are his brothers always like that?"

"No. Usually they're much worse."

Back at Martin's house, I turn the jetpacks on to get us up into his bedroom. The violin is still magically playing, but it stops the second we go into the room. (My "Pick up the slack, till Martin gets back" spell really worked.)

There's a knock on the bedroom door. "Martin? May I come in?" his mother asks.

Martin whispers, "Hide!" and I dive under the bed. It's dusty down here, and I come *this* close to sneezing. Martin opens the door and lets his mom in.

"I didn't want to interrupt you while you were practicing," she says. "But I've been listening all afternoon."

"Oh, really? Did I sound okay?"

"More than okay. Martin, you sounded fantastic!" she says.

"Uh. Thanks!"

My nose itches again. I pinch it with my fingers. Next time I have to hide in somebody's room, I'm going to try the closet. At least there'd be less dust.

Then Martin's mom tells him, "So I've decided you're ready. I just got off the phone with Maestro Chaliapin, and he's agreed to hear your audition next Saturday."

"But Mom! I need to practice a lot more!"

"No, from what I've heard today, you're ready. I'm so proud of you!" She gives him a big hug . . .

. . . and I sneeze.

She pulls away and puts her hand on his forehead. "You're not coming down with a cold, are you?"

"No! I'm fine! But I really don't want to audition!"

"Don't be silly."

After she leaves and the door is safely closed again, I scramble out from under the bed.

"You can't audition on Saturday," I say. "We've got the carnival!"

"Don't worry. On Saturday, I predict that I'll have the worst cold in the history of colds." Martin pretends to sneeze.

I suddenly feel a little guilty. "Are you sure you want to miss your big audition? You're really good."

Martin pretends to sneeze again. "But I've got this terrible, terrible cold." He smiles. "My mom will pull a few more strings and reschedule. She's good at that. So what do you and I have to do next?"

"I can't believe I'm saying this, but we're in great shape! Take tomorrow off!"

Wow, a whole day off! I've never been able to take a break in the middle of my assignment before. Maybe I'm getting better at this whole fairy godmother thing.

CHAPTER

27

When I get back to my house, Mom and Madison are in the backyard, gardening. For Mom, that means pulling weeds and trimming things; for Madison it means dancing around and pretending she's a ladybug.

"Did you have a good afternoon with Martin?" Mom asks me.

"Yes. We're going to put on a carnival to raise money for the school." Mom has to find out about it sometime, so I might as well tell her now.

"But I thought the carnival got canceled because of the flood."

"We're going to make the stuff ourselves," I say, leaving out the part where I use magic to make it.

"That's a great idea!" Mom says. "If you need any help, let me know."

Since I've got a magic wand, I won't need any help at all. But I just nod and tell Mom, "I sure will."

BEEP! BEEP! BEEP! is the first sound I hear when I open my bedroom door. It's a warning alert coming from three pink snowplows, each about the size of a Tonka trunk, that are shoveling the snow that's streaming from the portal.

It looks like Katarina's got things under control. Sort of; my room *is* colder than the walk-in freezer at the restaurant. Thick frost covers the windows, and icicles hang on the furniture. Not only that, there's a little igloo on my dresser. I lean down and peer into the igloo's entrance tunnel. "Katarina? Are you in there?"

Katarina crawls out wearing the pink sweater she's been knitting. (It's got special holes in the back so her wings can still stick out.) But the sweater's not doing much good—her teeth are chattering. "Where have you been?" she asks.

"Helping Martin," I say. "It's freezing in here! Mom's going to notice this for sure!"

Katarina pulls her sweater closer and shivers. "Only you and I can feel the cold. It's our own private winter. You might as well get used to it!"

"We don't need to get used to it. I've got a great plan! We're going to—"

Katarina says, in a peevish voice, "Why bother including me

now? I'm only your teacher. I've only sacrificed my entire life to be here in your room."

Oops. Maybe I should have taken her along this afternoon. "I'm sorry your feelings are hurt."

"My feelings aren't hurt. What makes you think my feelings are hurt?"

Her feelings are *definitely* hurt.

"Now, excuse me while I crawl into my igloo and stare at the wall."

Even though she's being way too dramatic, I sympathize. Once Sunny had a karate demonstration and didn't invite me. Later, I found out she thought I would be bored, but I would rather have been bored than left out. And that's probably what's going on with Katarina right now.

WHAM! My window slams up, and both Katarina and I jump at the sound.

WHIRRR! The Frisbee-unicycle I made at the zoo, which I've completely forgotten about, zooms through the window and heads straight for us.

We both shriek and dive out of the way.

CRASH! The spinning wheel of the Frisbee-unicycle knocks into Katarina's igloo and smashes it into a million pieces.

Then there's an angry little voice from my windowsill: "If you're going to make a flying unicycle, Lacey, you need to keep it under control!" It's Augustina, who's so mad that blue sparks are coming out of her fingertips.

Katarina flies up near my face. "Now what have you done?"

Augustina flies over, too, and snaps at Katarina. "You're her teacher. Why don't *you* know what she's done?"

"Because I've been too busy plowing snow! Who has time to teach?"

"Stop fighting, you guys," I say. "I tried to make a unicycle for the club at school, and it got away. I won't do it again."

They stop glaring at each other and instead they glare at me.

Augustina points at the Frisbee-unicycle, which is crashed on the other side of the dresser with its pedals still pedaling. "That misbegotten device you created was flying all over town."

Katarina is shocked. "Did anybody see it?"

Augustina shakes her head. "Thankfully, nobody human. Just three dogs, twelve crows, and a skunk."

Now that she mentions it, there *is* a skunky aroma wafting from the unicycle. That skunk must have been *scared*.

Augustina looks disgusted and tries to wave the smell away. "Alarms were sounding all over Godmother headquarters. It could have been the end of fairy godmothering as we know it!"

"I'm sorry! I'm sorry," I say. "The unicycle is here now. Everything's good!"

Augustina gives me a pinch. "One thing's not good. *You.* Make that two things. You and your teacher. Katarina!" Then she gives Katarina a pinch, too. "Keep your student under control, or we'll all pay the price!"

And she disappears out the window as fast as she came.

I decide it might be a good idea to give Katarina a little time to calm down, so I go lie on the couch in the family room—where it's warm—and watch *Bridemonsters* reruns. Julius curls up on my lap, purring.

Madison comes waltzing in, singing, "I'm a ladybug! I'm a ladybug. Tell me to fly away home!"

"All right. Madison, Madison, fly away home!"

"I *am* home! I tricked you!"

She falls on the couch next to me, giggling hysterically. Julius is used to her, so he doesn't even bother opening his eyes. (Is he a brave cat? Or just lazy?) Madison finally giggles herself out and says, "Mom and Dad are going to the restaurant, and you're gonna make me SpaghettiOs and then we'll wash Barbie's hair."

Nobody told me I was babysitting tonight. Normally I'd be annoyed, but every hour outside my room is an hour when I'm not getting yelled at by fairies. So instead of complaining, all I say to Madison is "Which Barbie?"

"All of them. And then we're going to watch *Ladybug and the Tramp.*"

"You mean *Lady and the Tramp*."

"No, we're going to turn the sound off and you're going to do ladybug voices."

I say, in a high, squeaky, sort-of-insect voice, "Hi, Tramp! I'm the ladybug of your dreams! Let's eat LadybugOs."

Madison laughs like she's never going to stop. To a five-year-old, anything in a high, squeaky voice is absolutely hilarious.

Mom and Dad get home, and I give Julius one last hug before I go back to my room. I tell him, "Maybe you can't feel the cold, but there's going to be a lot of yelling. Believe me, you're better off out here."

My bedroom is so quiet, you can almost hear the icicles forming. The magic unicycle has frozen solid, poor thing. It'll probably be really happy to turn back into a Frisbee at midnight.

Katarina has rebuilt her igloo bigger and better—it's an ig-mansion. She must have added fifty rooms! Dim, cold, blue light pours out of every window.

Shivering, I peer inside. Katarina is sound asleep on a little bed covered with white fur. (It had better be fake fur, I think to myself.)

Even with all the fur, fake or not, it doesn't exactly look warm and cozy in there. Plus it could be the most wonderful room in the world, and it would still vanish at the stroke of twelve.

Is that what Katarina's whole life has been like? Cold blue

rooms with no one, no family or friends or pets, to keep her company?

No wonder she's so cranky all the time. If she weren't a fairy godmother, I'd say she needed a fairy godmother.

CHAPTER

28

My eyes flutter open and I see morning sun streaming through arched, iron-framed windows. The kind of windows castles have.

"Katarina!" I say, not wanting to move from under my pile of covers. "What have you done now?"

When there's no answer from her, I sit up and look around. My bed is in the middle of a castle kitchen with stone walls and a ginormous fireplace. And there's a blond girl on her hands and knees scrubbing the filthy floor. A blond girl who's wearing a cheerleader's uniform.

"*Paige?* What are you doing here?" I ask.

She looks up with a scared expression. "Stepmother! I'm almost done! Please don't throw more food at me! I've done everything you asked!"

Stepmother? I look behind me, and there's nobody there.

Then I glance into the mirror on the wall and see myself. I've got fancy hair, and evil eyebrows, and my hands are full of green Jell-O.

Paige screams, "No! Not the Jell-O!"

I can't help myself. I throw it at her.

And then I wake up—I'm in my freezing-cold bedroom, with no trace of a castle or Paige.

Creepy dream! And how weird that I was the evil step-mother. I think about the dream for a while. In the food fight at school, Paige got dirty and the kids made fun of her. And it was my fault.

OMG! I'm the evil stepmother in real life, too!

I've got to make Paige understand how sorry I am. But I've already tried to apologize. What else can I do?

"I lost my shoe and you. I don't know what to doooooooooooooo!" I sing on Paige's front lawn.

That song doesn't sound familiar? It's from *Cinderella, the Rock Opera*.

That doesn't sound familiar, either? Well, it's a play that my school put on, and Paige had the lead role. The words from her big solo kind of fit what's going on between the two of us right now. Plus I'm hoping that the fact I'm humiliating myself on her lawn will make her feel better, or at least make her smile.

The song doesn't have that many words, but I sing them over

and over again at the top of my voice: *"I lost my shoe and you. I can't believe it's true. I don't know what to do. I'm feeling so very bluuuuuuuue."*

Katarina is in my pocket holding her ears. "This is a ridiculous plan! Stop that yowling before my eardrums explode!"

A moment later, Paige's front door opens, and I hold my breath, hoping that she'll come out smiling.

But it's not Paige. It's her father, Dr. Harrington, who's dressed for work at the hospital. "Hi, Lacey. Beautiful morning, isn't it?" he asks, and then he gets into his car and drives away without mentioning the singing.

I guess he just assumes that all twelve-year-old girls are a little crazy.

"She's not coming out! Let's go!" Katarina says.

But I launch into the song again: *"I lost my shoe and you . . ."*

Then Paige's door reopens and a girl comes out. It's *Makayla*!

This is worse than I thought. Paige has unfriended me and refriended Makayla!

Makayla walks up, puts her arm around me, and raises her cell phone. She speaks in her very-important-news-blogger voice: "I'm here with Lacey Unger-Ware, who has been quite the girl about town lately. I don't know how she does it. *Now* she's outside Paige Harrington's house singing a song. Come on, Lacey! Show us what you can do."

I hesitate. If she posts the video, I'm going to look like a total idiot. But then I remember that's the whole point of what I'm doing. To get your friend back, you have to be willing to put yourself on the line. The really embarrassing line.

So, as Makayla records me, I open my mouth and sing, *"I—"*

"STOP!" Paige shouts, so loud that Makayla jumps and drops her phone. As she leans down to pick it up, Paige yanks me inside the house and shuts the door.

We take turns peering through the curtains at Makayla, who knocks for a while but finally gives up and walks away.

I turn to Paige and jump right into my apology. "Paige! I messed up with Martin and you, and I'm soooooo sorry!" I launch back into the song. *"I lost my shoe and you . . ."*

"Wait! Will you do one thing for me?" Paige asks.

"Sure! Anything!"

"Never sing that song again!"

"But I need to show you how sorry I am."

"I got that! Stop! I forgive you!"

"You *do*?"

Paige nods. "Anybody who would do something that silly deserves a second chance."

Katarina pokes her head out of my pocket, surprised. "She *does*? I told her to buy you jewelry!"

"No, the song is enough. More than enough."

I give Paige a big hug. "You forgive me! You forgive me! I'm so happy."

But I'm only happy for a moment more, because then Paige says, in a very serious voice, "There's a big, big problem. Let me tell you why Makayla was here."

I don't like the sound of that.

The more I hear, the worse it gets. After Paige finishes talking, I text Sunny and Martin: *EMERGENCY! FOUNTAIN PARK ASAP!*

CHAPTER 29

At the park, I turn to Paige. "Tell Sunny and Martin what you told me."

Paige takes a deep breath and starts talking. "First thing this morning, Makayla came over to my house and started asking me all sorts of questions about Lacey. She knew Lacey and I had a fight and thought I would be happy to badmouth her."

"What did she want to know?" Martin asks.

Paige says, "About the fairy godmother dress. And about backpacks with pink sparkles coming out of them. And . . . about whether I believed in magic."

Katarina moans. "She asked about *magic*? This is bad! This is really bad."

Martin says, "Makayla must have thought about it last night and decided there was more to the story than smelly cleaning products. Maybe she's a real reporter after all."

Sunny asks, "So what did you say back, Paige?"

"I pretended like I thought she was joking. I told her if she was going to punk me for her blog, she was going to have to try harder. Then *she* pretended like that's what she was doing and left."

Martin nods. "She who punks last punks best. Paige, you're *maar.*"

Katarina shudders. "Stop with the Elvish! Your accent is horrible. With that pronunciation, you just called Paige a jelly doughnut."

I try to put the discussion back on track. "Anyway, I think we're okay—Makayla doesn't really know anything."

Katarina says. "She knows enough. You can forget about your carnival."

Sunny says, "There's going to be a carnival?"

"Yes!" I say. "That's the new plan. I'm going to make a magic carnival with rides and stuff to pay for the after-school programs."

Katarina shakes her head. "Not with Makayla watching you! Magic—of any kind—is too dangerous. Fairy godmothers survive with humans because humans don't pay attention to anything. But now *Makayla is paying attention.*"

Martin looks confused. "Wait—I've got a fairy godmother who can't use magic?"

"What if Lacey does magic without making it *look* like

magic? A carnival that seems like the kids made it, but it's really all from Lacey's wand?" Sunny asks.

Katarina shakes her head again. "Even that would be too dangerous with Makayla sticking her nosy little nose into everything. All she needs is one glimpse of Lacey's wand in action, and it's all over."

I feel like screaming. "We've got to have the carnival," I say. "What can we do?"

Katarina looks wise and solemn. "We need to take care of Makayla."

"Take care of her, how?" I ask.

"I suggest the Red Shoes Protocol."

Paige looks intrigued. (She loves shoes.) "What's that?"

Katarina smiles. "Simple, really. We give her beautiful dancing shoes. She puts them on . . . and she dances away, never to be seen again."

"But what happens to her?" Sunny asks.

"Well, in the Middle Ages they usually danced into the woods and were eaten by wolves. But it doesn't have to be wolves. Coyotes, mountain lions. Even a pack of little yappy dogs would work. At any rate, your problem is solved and we can go on with the carnival."

"No way! We can't send Makayla off to be eaten by wolves," I almost shout.

Katarina shrugs. "Fine. Go with the yappy dogs. They're small but mean."

"No! I'm not going to send Makayla off to be eaten by anything."

Katarina says, "Well, then. There's only one thing I can say. If Makayla stays . . . we're DOOMED!"

We sit around like we're having a contest for who can look the most miserable. I think I win, because I'm the one who's wrecking Martin's life, not to mention mine and Katarina's. I'm so over being a fairy godmother! Sure, I've got a magic wand, but does that make things easier? No! It only messes things up. For all the good it does me, I'd be better off trying to do things without any magic at all.

But I could never raise the money we need without magic. Could I?

And then I have my best blinking-lightbulb-idea moment so far. I say, "We can do it!"

"We can do what?" Sunny asks.

"We can put on a *real* carnival this weekend. Without magic! It will take a lot of work, but we can do it!"

"Nonsense!" Katarina says. "An enterprise this big must have magic!"

But Sunny, Paige, Martin, and I talk, and we talk, and we talk some more.

An hour later, we've got a carnival planned.

A *non*-magic carnival, and Makayla won't be able to do a thing about that. By the time we're done talking, even Katarina looks less depressed.

"Well . . . it might work," she says. "But wolves or yappy dogs would be a lot easier."

"You really think Principal Conehurst will let us do it?" Martin asks me.

I nod. *"Absolutely!"*

CHAPTER 30

"*Impossible!* You won't even be able to get the flyers done by Friday, much less put together a whole carnival," Principal Conehurst tells me and Martin in his office.

If Katarina were in my pocket right now, she'd be whispering, "I told you so!" Luckily, she stayed home to supervise portal snow removal.

"We can do it!" I say. "We're desperate! People hate Martin, and we need them to stop hating Martin. The only way to do that is to fix the water tower and get back the field trips. Martin can barely take it anymore."

"I think I can only take it till Sunday when the moon is full," Martin says.

The principal raises an eyebrow. "Don't tell me—you're a werewolf."

Martin shakes his head. "No, it's worse than that! I'm unpopular! And not just a little unpopular. *Hugely* unpopular. People throw food at me!"

Principal Conehurst gives Martin a sympathetic look. "I get what you're saying. But organizing an entire carnival in five days is completely unrealistic."

"We can do it," I say.

The door bursts open, and Mrs. Fleecy races in. "*Please* let them do it!"

Principal Conehurst looks at her, startled.

"I admit it," Mrs. Fleecy says. "I was listening on the intercom, and I think the carnival is a lovely idea. Maybe they'll raise the money, or maybe they won't. But the important thing is that this school will start pulling together again. I've worked here for almost twenty years, and I've never seen so many unhappy students. At least let Lacey and Martin try."

"But a carnival in five days?"

"What better way to make the kids forget their problems and work together? Give them a month, and they'll bicker and fight. Give them five days, and they'll have to be a team."

Principal Conehurst frowns, thinking. "But the school has no funds for this. And remember, all the carnival supplies were ruined."

"We don't need any funds! And we'll bring our own supplies," I say.

More frowning from the principal. "Let's be logical. Because of the flood, you don't even have booths."

"Thought of that!" Martin says. "We'll go to every store that sells refrigerators and ask them for the boxes. My Cub Scout troop did that for our haunted Halloween house."

"Cardboard boxes? Won't that be kind of . . . bare?"

Mrs. Fleecy says, "That's a perfect job for Craft-N-Crunch! And I've got a garage full of paint!"

"What about lights? On Friday night it will be dark."

I say, "There are lights in the parking lot."

And Martin adds, "And every kid could bring in one strand of Christmas tree lights from home."

Mrs. Fleecy smiles. "That would be *pretty*!"

"How about rides?" Wow. Principal Conehurst thinks of everything. Luckily, we have, too.

Martin says, "I've got a basement full of tools. There's just going to be one ride, really. I'm going to build it, and it's going to be epic!"

Even I don't know what Martin's got planned for the ride. All he'll tell me is that he's got it under control. I just hope it's not *too* epic.

Principal Conehurst is still thinking. "What about prizes for the games?"

Hmmm. We *didn't* think of everything. We'd need money to buy prizes. All those stuffed animals . . . and then I grin. "I have at least ten stuffed animals in my closet that I never look at. And I bet that every other girl in school does, too. The prizes will be donated."

The principal looks at me, Martin, and Mrs. Fleecy (who's giving him a thumbs-up and waggling her eyebrows like a crazy person). He crosses his arms and frowns.

OMG. He's going to tell us no. Antarctica, here I come!

Then he reaches over and grabs the microphone for the school's public address system. "Attention, Lincoln Middle School students! Please join Martin Shembly and Lacey Unger-Ware for a meeting in the parking lot this afternoon after school. They are organizing a fund-raising carnival to be held this weekend. The proceeds will go to restoring the field trips and the water tower. Also, Mrs. Fleecy will provide cookies for everyone. That is all."

He waggles his eyebrows back at Mrs. Fleecy.

CHAPTER

31

After my last class, I stash my books and race down the hall. There's so much to do, and only four afternoons to do it in!

Just as I turn the corner, I see Scott, who's about to go through the double doors that lead to the parking lot. "Hey!" I call.

He stops and waits until I catch up. "So *that's* what you and Martin were doing this weekend. Working on the carnival idea."

Well, if you leave out all the time we spent riding magic jetpacks, that *is* what we were doing, so I just nod. Then I remember that Martin's supposed to get all the credit, so I add, "It was Martin's idea, really. I knew he was smart, but he's so talented, and organized, and . . . he's just great!"

There's a funny look in Scott's eyes. I guess I *am* overdoing it a little bit. "You like him, don't you?" he asks.

Is Scott jealous? He couldn't be. After all, he told his little brothers I'm not his girlfriend as fast as the words would come out of his mouth.

Then Scott says, "Martin sounds pretty great. I can see why you'd rather hang out with him."

O.

M.

G.

Scott *is* jealous! It doesn't mean he's my boyfriend—but maybe it means that he would mind if Martin was my boyfriend. (Does that make sense? You know what I mean, right?)

Am I shallow if I think that's *awesome*?

So now I need to figure out a way to let Scott know that Martin and I absolutely don't like each other that way. Not at all.

But before I get a chance, Martin races down the hall, waving at me wildly. "Lacey! I've been looking for you! Let's go!"

Scott stares as Martin takes me by the hand and drags me through the door . . .

. . . and we *instantly* get pounced on by Makayla and Taylor, whose camera is already raised.

"Here is the carnival couple now," Makayla says in her fake-sounding newswoman voice. "Will they convince the school to go along with their plan? My sources say the kids aren't liking it so far."

Eek.

———

Luckily, Makayla's "sources" are wrong. (I think Makayla had exactly two: herself and Taylor.)

Makayla probably thought the kids would be so busy being mad at Martin that they wouldn't want to help, but over a hundred volunteers show up in the parking lot ready to work. I guess they want the carnival more than they want to hate Martin.

To my complete surprise, everyone treats me and Martin like we know what we're doing. They listen to us when we talk, and Blaine Anders even laughs at one of Martin's jokes. Now all we have to do is put on a complete carnival without using any magic.

Gulp.

But I don't have time to worry. I've got too much to do! We break the kids into teams:

Team One: Booths.

Team Two: Decorations and lights.

Team Three: Games and prizes.

Team Four: Food.

Team Five: Signs, flyers, and advertising.

It's a lot of teams, but we've got a lot of kids, and we have no problem filling the teams up. So far so good.

Okay, I do have a little time to worry. And what I worry about is Makayla. She and Taylor tell everyone they're filming a long news report about the carnival, but I'm the only person they're filming. And every once in a while I look up and see Makayla staring right at me. I'm totally sure her "news report" isn't about the carnival, it's about catching me doing magic. Since I'm not tossing a single spell, Makayla can't prove a thing. But that doesn't stop me from feeling scared every time I see the camera pointed in my direction.

Monday night, I get a text from Martin: *My mom was mad I got home late.*

I text back: *Everything okay?*

Martin: *I'm grounded till I turn 30.*

Me: *What about the carnival?*

Martin: *If you can come over and do the magic violin spell every day, I'll work on the ride in the basement while I'm "practicing" in my room.*

Me: *No prob. Give me a hint about the ride you're working on.*

Martin: *It's a surprise! Just wait.*

The zip line was also a surprise. I sure hope this is a better one.

Over the next few days, the carnival really starts to come together. It's the most planning I've ever had to do. It's bigger than a school play. It's bigger than a wedding. It's just—*big.*

Katarina stays home to supervise the little snowplows; she really needs to, because every day the portal in the room gets bigger. When she's not chanting spells to make pink snowplows, she's swearing under her breath in something that sounds like

Elvish. I'll have to remember some of the words if I ever get mad at Martin.

The week is so much work. Every single day, I'm tempted to use just a little, teeny, itsy-bitsy bit of magic. But every single day, I also see Makayla and Taylor skulking around watching me. You know those TV shows where the creepy reporters try to talk to famous people outside restaurants? Makayla and Taylor are just like that.

So no magic, just lots of help from the kids at school. And I'm learning things about my classmates I never knew:

Marcie Dunphy, the smallest girl in the sixth grade, can make any kind of balloon animals you can think of. Not just poodles and giraffes, but meerkats and iguanas.

Gaby Thompson, who talks more than any kid I've ever met, is a stuffed-animal maniac, and she donates ninety-seven stuffed animals from her personal collection. (I get the feeling there are still a lot of animals at home.) I wonder if she talks to the animals at night when there's no one else around.

Dylan Hernandez knows an insane amount about junk food. His family owns an industrial kettle-corn maker and a cotton-candy machine that they're lending to the carnival. And since Mom and Dad say they'll donate a huge batch of caramel apples, there's going to be plenty to eat.

And Scott is so good at untangling Christmas lights, it's almost spooky. (Dad should hire him next Christmas.) But no matter how friendly I am, Scott never has much to say to me. Here's how it always goes when I walk by him and one of his piles of lights:

Me: "Hi, Scott!"

Scott: "Hi, Lacey."

(Seemingly endless silence.)

Me: "Bye, Scott."

Scott: "Bye, Lacey."

The first time we have this "conversation," I tell myself he's busy. By the fifth time, I'm pretty sure it's because he's mad at me about Martin. Or . . . maybe he's *not* mad at me about Martin. Maybe he just doesn't care about me at all.

Sigh. Being a fairy godmother and having an almost-boyfriend don't mix.

Except for my seemingly endless silences with Scott, the week is so busy, it's kind of a blur. Principal Conehurst says we can't miss a minute of classes, so we all work like crazy before school, during lunch, and after school. Kids even work during passing periods. Sometimes all they do is paint one flower on a cardboard booth, but it sure adds up.

Every afternoon, I bike over to Martin's house, being super extra careful to make sure that Makayla isn't following me. Then I cast the magic violin spell so it sounds like Martin is practicing instead of working on the top-secret ride he's designing for the carnival. He still won't tell me what it is! I try looking in the basement window to see what's going on down there, but he's taped newspaper over the glass.

Late Thursday afternoon, I walk around the parking lot—excuse me, *carnival*—making notes about what we have to finish tomorrow. There's a lot on the list, but things are looking okay so far. The booths are in place, the lights are strung, and the tables for food have been set up.

Just as I'm leaving, the sun breaks through the white, puffy clouds overhead. I hope it's a good sign.

CHAPTER

32

Mom is clattering around in the kitchen when I get home, so I stick my head in the door. "I'm back!"

There's a huge bowl of apples on the table, and Mom stirs a giant pot of caramel sauce on the stove. Julius sits on her feet hoping something tasty will come his way.

"Hi, Lacey!" Mom says. "It's almost dipping time. I need an assistant."

"Let me put my stuff in my room and I'll be right back."

As I'm leaving, Madison skips into the kitchen. "Mom! Can we have fish sticks for dinner?"

"You don't even like fish sticks," Mom says.

"But Prince Cornelius Sebastian loves them."

"Who's Prince Cornelius Sebastian?"

"My new penguin friend."

Mom is used to Madison's imaginary friends. "Tell your penguin friend I'll consider it."

Madison smiles and skips away.

When I open the door to my room, I'm hit by an icy blast of cold air. It's lucky that Mom, Dad, and Madison can't feel this, but I sure can. By the time I make it to my bed, head down in the wind, my fingers and toes are numb.

The little snowplows are busily clearing the snow from the portal, which is now almost two feet wide. The portal has grown a lot since this morning, but so far the plows are doing a great job.

There's no sign of Katarina, so I peer into one of the frosty windows of her ig-mansion and see her sitting by a tiny, roaring fireplace. She's wrapped in a heavy blanket, drinking hot chocolate, and looking very comfortable.

"Stop rubbernecking!" Katarina snaps. "Do you know how disconcerting it is to have a giant eyeball staring in through your window?"

I consider sticking my tongue out at her, but I'm afraid it will freeze to the glass. "The carnival is looking really good," I tell her. "And Mom and I are making caramel apples."

Katarina perks up. "If you're making poison ones, I have a great recipe. The secret's in the wolfsbane. Always fresh, never frozen."

Katarina is seriously disturbing sometimes.

As I fight my way back out of the room through the icy wind, I notice that the door to the bathroom I share with Madison is open. I pull it closed and keep going.

When I step back into the hallway, I nearly knock over Madison, who's dragging her plastic kiddie pool in from the backyard.

"What are you doing?" I ask.

"Nothing."

"You're doing something. What's the pool for?"

"For my penguin."

"Your imaginary penguin doesn't need a pool. Take it back outside."

"He's not imaginary. He's real! I'm going to give him fish sticks for dinner. They're his favorite."

I'm about to take the pool away when I hear a strange sound inside her room. It sounds like . . .

Eaeyeeeap.

OMG!

I squeeze past the pool, open Madison's door, and stare inside. Staring back at me is a two-foot-tall, black-and-white penguin with an orange bill.

Eaeyeeeap, he squawks.

He's definitely real.

I pull Madison inside and close the door. The penguin gives me a curious look and then waddles over and tries to eat my shoelaces.

Madison puts her hands on her hips. "You've got Julius, and now I've got Prince Cornelius Sebastian. Isn't he the *cutest*?"

"But where did he come from?"

"He was in the bathroom. Finders keepers—he's mine!"

I sit on Madison's bed, trying to figure out what's going on. Could Prince Cornelius Sebastian have wandered in from my room? How could that happen? All I know for sure is that, no matter what, Madison can*not* have a pet penguin.

The penguin gives up trying to eat my shoelaces and looks at me with one eye. *Eaeyeeeap! Eaeyeeeap!* I've got to get him back in my room where, I hope, Katarina can help me get rid of him.

Madison rummages through her costume box. "*I* can speak Penguin! He's saying, 'I want a pink tutu!'"

Geez. She's planning tutus, which for Madison means they're already best friends forever. Getting him away is not going to be easy.

"Ooh, and a hat, too!" Madison says as she pulls one out. What am I going to tell her?

My mind is blank, and then I see a black-and-white dog figurine on Madison's windowsill, one of the puppies from *101 Dalmatians*. I kneel down by Madison, very serious. "I'm going to tell you a secret. You can't keep Prince Cornelius Sebastian."

"He's mine! I finders-keepers-ed him!"

"But he's in terrible danger. Life-and-death danger!"

Madison looks at me, interested despite herself.

"There's a girl at my school named Makayla. She's beautiful but evil. And you know what she wants more than anything else in the whole world?"

"What?"

"She wants a coat made from penguins."

Madison crosses her arms. "A *coat*? That's in a movie."

This is my make-or-break moment, and I choose my words carefully. "That's where the evil Makayla got the idea. I need to take Prince Cornelius Sebastian to the zoo, so he'll be safe."

"I don't believe you. You're making this up," Madison says.

Suddenly, from the bathroom, there's an evil cackle. Madison and I both jump.

"Did you do that?" Madison asks, with terror on her face.

I shake my head—and then the cackle comes again.

Madison throws her arms in the air and runs out of the room shrieking louder than any little girl has ever shrieked.

Katarina flies into the room from the bathroom, covering her ears. "That girl should be a car alarm." She flies behind the penguin and cackles again. The penguin runs, terrified, into the bathroom. I follow him through the bathroom and into my freezing bedroom, where he hops through the portal and disappears into the snowy wilderness that's on the other side.

Katarina flies up to me as I stand in my room, shivering. "Where'd you learn to laugh like that?" I ask.

"The same place I learned the recipe for the poison apples." She yells after the penguin, "Run, you little monster, run!"

She really *does* hate penguins.

"Katarina, you said that only you and I can see the portal or Antarctica. But Madison saw Prince Cornelius Sebastian."

She points at the wide-open wall of my bedroom. "This may be a magic portal to the South Pole, but that penguin was real. Portals work both ways, just like a door does, which explains how that foul fowl got in here. When the full moon comes—two nights from now—the magic portal will close. And if you don't complete your assignment with Martin, we'll be on the other side."

"We can't have penguins wandering around the house!"

"I've got a solution for that."

I expect her to raise her wand and toss a spell. Instead, she gives me a smug look and says, "Keep the door closed, you ninny."

And right then, my bedroom door opens. Katarina darts out of sight as Mom comes into the room, holding a caramel-covered wooden spoon. Even though there's a vast Antarctic wilderness visible through a two-foot portal on the other side of the room, Mom doesn't see it.

"Lacey Unger-Ware!" Mom says. "What did you say to your sister? She's scared to death!"

"I'm sorry. I was just telling her a fairy tale about an evil girl and a penguin."

"Don't do it again. And you're supposed to be helping me with the apples."

I find Madison in the family room and whisper, "Prince Cornelius Sebastian is safe. He's already at the zoo."

"And the evil Makayla is gone?"

"Yes."

Madison breathes a sigh of relief and heads into the kitchen. "Mom? I don't want fish sticks for dinner anymore."

CHAPTER

33

Not much classwork gets done at Lincoln Middle School on Friday. Who can concentrate on math or French or World Cultures when there's a carnival in just a few hours? We open to the paying public at five o'clock sharp!

Somehow, we all make it through the day. The teachers aren't too hard on us—I think they're looking forward to the carnival, too.

When the last bell rings, a hundred kids swarm the parking lot to put on the finishing touches. I find Martin and ask, "Is your top-secret ride ready?"

"Yes! I'm on my way home to get it right now. Wait'll you see it!"

"Do you need me to come do the magic violin spell?"

"No—my mom's working late today."

"Okay! Come back as fast as you can!"

And by four forty-five, except for Martin's secret ride, the carnival is ready to go. Sunny, Paige, and I stand back and take just a moment to admire everything.

"It's good!" Sunny says.

Paige nods. "Who needs magic, anyway?"

We sure don't—because just then Scott plugs in the Christmas lights. (He may be giving me the silent treatment, but that doesn't stop him from being a hard worker.) There are thousands of colored, twinkling bulbs. And, suddenly, we've got a carnival.

The booths look great. Sure, they're just made out of boxes, but with paint and bright lights, they don't look like cardboard at all. The stuffed-animal prizes are piled in pyramids by the game booths, and you'd never know that they were slightly used.

Tables are heaped high with food for sale. It's not just the caramel apples, the kettle corn, and the cotton candy I was expecting—there are also cookies, cupcakes, chocolate-covered pretzels, and fudge that parents sent in. (A lot of people were busy cooking last night.) There's even a platter of beef jerky; it's Marcie Dunphy's dad's specialty.

And Makayla and Taylor are *still* stalking me with the camera. I should be used to it by now, but this is getting really old. Makayla is so sure I'm using magic, she's not going to stop till she proves it.

Makayla watches as Principal Conehurst walks up to Sunny, Paige, and me with a big smile on his face. "I didn't think it was possible to do this in five days, but you guys pulled it off!" He glances up at the dark clouds overhead. "And the weatherman says it's not supposed to rain until Sunday, so that shouldn't be a problem. I guess all that's left is to see how much money you kids raise."

"It's going to be a lot," I tell him, and Sunny and Paige nod.

"It's going to have to be, if you're going to pay for both the water tower and the field trips. Still . . . this looks terrific. I don't want to jinx things, but I think this just might work."

Makayla butts in. "Principal Conehurst? Do you really think we can get the field trips back if the carnival makes a lot of money?"

He nods. "With a little luck."

Makayla's eyes shine. "I can go to the Online News Association banquet!"

All of a sudden, I realize something: going to the banquet really, really means a lot to her. I always thought Makayla was just a mean girl, but she has her dreams, too.

Makayla pushes down Taylor's camera. "Stop filming! We've got to get people here to buy tickets!" Makayla types something into her phone, and, a second later, every other phone in the parking lot, including mine, chirps with a text from her: *Carnival tonight! Spread the word!*

Makayla and Taylor scurry away, ready to tell the world.

The principal looks around and asks me, "Where's Martin's epic carnival ride?"

"He should be here anytime now," I say.

Then there's a shout from a megaphone: "Hey, everybody! Hey! Hey!"

We all turn and see Martin, dressed in the same gray coveralls he wore when he zip-lined off the water tower. The yellow bicycle helmet is back on his head, and he pulls a wagon that's covered with a tarp.

I run up to him, suddenly feeling very, very nervous. "Martin! What are you doing?" I whisper.

He whispers back, "I had a jetpack breakthrough. You helped me, actually."

"How?"

"When we flew to Abner's, I analyzed how they worked."

"That was *magic*!"

"But the aerodynamic concepts were correct! I've made a working prototype—and with only *three* leaf blowers!"

As more and more kids gather around, he whips the tarp off the wagon to reveal three leaf blowers strapped together with shiny silver duct tape. He picks up the megaphone. "The future of transportation is here, now. Tonight you can take a ride on a real, live jetpack! Kids only—grown-ups are too heavy! Five dollars a ride!"

Principal Conehurst pushes through the crowd. "Martin, that's way too dangerous!"

Martin quickly buckles on his homemade jetpack. "It's not dangerous at all. Everybody—WATCH THIS."

He flips a switch, and the leaf blowers on his back turn on with a roar. Blue exhaust smoke streams out toward the ground . . .

. . . and Martin rises into the air. Just a couple of feet, but he *is* floating above the ground.

This is amazing! He's really, really done it! He's not using tricks, he's not using magic. He's using something he invented himself!

The kids all applaud and cheer, and Martin gives a big wave. This is probably the best moment of his life.

As Martin hovers, he starts to turn around in a circle faster and faster. At first I think he's just showing off for the crowd— and then I notice that Martin looks queasy, like he's getting dizzy from spinning.

"Martin! It's time to come down!" I shout.

"I'm trying!" he shouts back.

Principal Conehurst makes a grab for him, but it's too late. Martin spins away like a wobbly, out-of-control top.

He whirls over the food tables, his feet knocking into every-thing. Sweets go flying, and kids have to duck so they don't get hit by flying caramel apples.

Next, spinning even faster, he hurtles through the pyramid of prizes. (Is spurtles a word? If it isn't, it should be.) Stuffed bears, tigers, and rabbits go flying, too.

Martin spurtles toward the row of cardboard carnival booths, and kids dive out of the way. This is going to be horrible! I've got to stop this now! I pull my wand out of my pocket, ready to toss a spell—and then I see Makayla and Taylor standing right in front of me, filming everything.

If I use magic on Martin, it'll be uploaded to YouTube before you can say "end of fairy godmothering as we know it."

I put my wand back in my pocket and watch in horror as Martin plows through the cardboard carnival booths like a bowling ball knocking down pins. And if this were bowling, he just got a strike.

When the last carnival booth is flattened, Martin whirls out of control toward the still-standing legs of the water tower.

WHUMP! He knocks into the spindly legs. *CRASH!* The legs collapse onto the school parking lot.

With a final blast of smelly blue smoke, the jetpack turns off and Martin drops to the ground.

Sunny, Paige, and I are the first ones to reach him. "Martin! Are you all right?" I say.

He sits up. "I'm fine! I'm fine!" He stands up, staggering and dizzy from all the spinning. He looks over at the carnival, which is now just a flattened pile of cardboard. "We can fix this!" he says. "We just all need to pitch in, and it'll be good as new!"

There's a rumble of thunder in the distance, as if somebody up there's laughing at him, and then it starts to rain. Not gentle, little drops, either. It's a cloudburst, with water pouring out of the sky in broad, wet sheets.

The kids run for cover, trampling the cardboard underfoot. The food melts into sugary sludge, and the bright paint washes away into the gutters.

Along with all our hopes.

CHAPTER
34

I walk into the Hungry Moose, wet and cold from the rain. I could have gone straight home, but I'm depressed enough already without getting yelled at for being a total failure as a fairy godmother.

Which I am.

In the kitchen, Dad has six sauté pans going at once on the range, and Madison is sitting at the table playing her Sparkle Pony game. Dad sees me and says, "Why aren't you at the carnival?"

"It got rained out."

Dad gives me a sympathetic look. "Bummer. Get that wet coat off and come stand by the oven."

When I walk over and stand with my back to the heat, Dad says, "You can try again tomorrow."

"Everything got knocked over and ruined."

"Oh, I'm so sorry. Maybe you guys can try it again next month."

I can't tell Dad that I'll be at the South Pole, so I just say, "Yeah, maybe."

Mom comes in carrying an empty tray. "Lacey! Why—"

"The rain wiped out the carnival," Dad says.

"Oh, honey," Mom says. She puts down the tray and gives me a big hug. "After all your hard work, too. Sometimes life just isn't fair."

Dad puts down his spatula and adds a hug of his own. Madison runs over to us. "I want to hug, too!" She wriggles in and hugs me tight.

A family hug is the best, and I wish this moment would never end.

But moments always end, and so does this one. While we're still hugging, the vegetables on the stove start splattering, and the bell that means somebody came in through the front door chimes, and the Sparkle Ponies start neighing on Madison's iPad, wanting her to pay attention to the game.

I hang on to everybody tight, but they all pull away. Dad goes back to the stove, Mom rushes into the dining room, and Madison runs back over to the table and starts tapping the iPad.

I bet I'm not going to be getting many hugs at the South Pole.

———

When we all get home from the restaurant, I go to my room and open the door . . .

. . . and find a blizzard inside my room.

I'm not talking about a snowstorm like the bad one we had last winter.

Or a fun, animated blizzard like the one in *Rudolph, the Red-Nosed Reindeer.*

I'm talking about a BLIZZARD, capital B, capital everything. There's so much snow that it looks like a swirling mass of white.

It takes all my might, and a couple of tries, to finally slam the door shut.

Oops. Shutting the door might have been a mistake. Because now I'm lost in a snowy, freezing wilderness. I pull out my wand, but what should I do? Make a torch? A tent? A toboggan? Suddenly, through the spiraling snow, I hear barking sounds and Katarina shouting, "Get away from me, you brutes!"

I stumble toward the sounds—and find Katarina surrounded by five big, angry leopard seals, which must have come in through the portal just like the penguin did. Only they aren't cute like Prince Cornelius Sebastian; they're scary-mean-looking. Hungry-looking, too. One of them has even taken a gigantic bite out of the top of her ig-mansion.

"Katarina! I'm here!"

"Do something! My wand's still in the igloo and my wings have iced up! Do anything! *But do it now!*"

The hungry leopard seals notice I'm standing here, and now a couple of them start waddling toward me. Eek! I raise my wand and chant, "Before we become meals, make toys out of seals!" I toss the spell, and there are five bright flashes of light. Instead of five live seals, there are five fluffy seal toys sitting in the snow. They'd be really cute, except they still have mean, angry expressions on their fuzzy embroidered faces.

Katarina is so cold that she's turned icy pale. I reach down and pick her up, very gently so I don't break her frozen wings.

I fight my way through the blizzard into my closet and shut the door behind me. It's icy even in here, but at least there's no wind.

I raise my wand and chant, "Cozy warmth we desire; make a magic campfire!" After I toss the spell, a small, crackling campfire appears on the snowy floor of my closet. I put Katarina down next to it, and she stretches out her shivering hands. It takes a few moments for her to go back to her normal pink. Finally, she turns to me and says, "That's what our lives are going to be like every day. So *please* tell me the carnival went well."

"Uh . . . actually . . . Martin smashed it. Then it got wrecked in the rain. It's canceled."

Katarina frowns for a minute; then she calls, "Seals! Come

eat me now and put me out of my misery!" She sounds like she means it.

"We still have one day left, Katarina! There must be something we can do!"

Katarina takes a deep breath. "You're right. I'm your teacher, and this is a teachable moment."

"That's better. So what do you want to teach me?"

"We're DOOOOOOOMED!!!"

"This is so unfair! I never asked to be a fairy godmother! I just wanted to be a normal kid! Normal kids don't get sent to Antarctica when they fail at something—they get sent to their rooms. Their blizzard-free rooms! I would *love* to be sent to my room!"

"Oh, poor you. Boo-hoo-hoo. Life is so unfair. I've spent my whole life helping people get their dreams, and what do I get? An igloo. Will any of them care that I'm banished? No! They don't even send me cards on my birthday. At least your friends and your family will miss you when you're gone. Me? Who cares?"

That's super depressing. No wonder Katarina's so cranky all the time. If we ever get out of this, I'm going to have to remember to do something nice for her. *But first we have to get out this!* "Katarina, you've got to help me! Tell me what to do! You're my teacher!"

"I'm a fairy godmother teacher. We don't help. We don't tell you what to do. We don't even give gold stars!"

"So what *do* fairy godmother teachers do?" I ask.

"My old teacher, Terrifica Fata, believed in the three Rs. Rant, roar, and ridicule."

"Well, your old teacher sounds *horrible*."

Katarina looks around the closet nervously. "Shhh!! Terrifica has very big ears. Wherever she is, she's probably listening!"

"Wait a minute," I say. "Her name is Terrifica? That means *terrifying* in Latin."

Katarina stares at me. "How do you know that?"

"Abner told me! He's got a mini carnival at his house, and he named the mini roller coaster The Terrifica because it's so scary."

Katarina stares at me. "You're sure? He really, truly used the word *Terrifica?*'"

I nod.

Then she says something I never, ever thought I'd hear coming out of her mouth: *"OMG!"*

CHAPTER 35

Splurch! Splurch! Splurch!

Katarina and I are inside a giant pumpkin, and it's *rolling.*

Ew! It's so gross in here. Stringy orange pumpkin innards and seeds tumble all around us. "*Why* didn't you let me make us jetpacks?" I ask Katarina.

"Pumpkin carriages are the traditional way to travel—only you're supposed to transform the pumpkin into an actual carriage, you numbskull!" And then a giant pumpkin seed hits her on the head and she goes flying.

THWUNK! The pumpkin hits something, hard, and splits open.

We're right at Abner's front door, completely covered in pumpkin goo. Katarina is so buried in gunk that I can't even see her.

Abner opens the door a moment later, and his mouth drops open when he sees the mess on his porch.

I figure I have about thirty seconds before he closes the door and calls the cops (or his psychiatrist), so I start talking, loud and fast. "Abner, you said nobody was going to give me and Martin a handout. But somebody gave *you* a handout."

Right then, Katarina digs her way out of the orange slime. "And her name was Terrifica Fata! Your very own fairy godmother! That's right, isn't it? Right? Right?"

"And that's why you named the little roller coaster after her," I add.

Abner leans against the door frame like he's feeling a little unsteady on his feet. After a long, long pause, he nods yes. "I've been keeping Terrifica Fata a secret for fifty-four years. She made my dream come true."

"Your dream was about pickles?" I ask.

"No, no! My dream was to get away from my uncle's horrible cucumber farm. She showed up one night, screeching at me about what an idiot I was." (Hmm . . . she sounds a lot like Katarina.) "She didn't stop screeching until I invented the recipe for the best darn pickles that anyone had ever tasted. It changed my life, not to mention making me rich. I couldn't have done it without her help."

I say, "And now Martin Shembly needs help! Big, big help! And he needs it before the full moon on Sunday morning!"

Abner looks at Katarina and says, "But he's got a fairy godmother. How much more help does he need?"

I tell him, "She's not his fairy godmother, *I* am!" Right then I slip in the pumpkin ooze and fall on my butt.

Abner extends a hand and pulls me up. "You two had better come in and tell me all about it."

He wipes pumpkin goo off his hand. "And can one of you please do a spell so you don't track pumpkin all over my nice clean carpet?"

Inside Abner's office, I take the miniature pickle carnival off the shelf and put it on his desk. I tell him, "Tomorrow morning, I want to use magic to turn this carnival big and real. And I want to tell everybody that the big and real carnival is yours, and that Martin Shembly talked you into donating it."

"People are supposed to believe that I just happened to have a carnival lying around?"

"We'll say that it's part of your collection, and that you had it stored in the barn. All you did was have some workmen wheel it out and set it up."

"The carnival is going to be *here*?"

"People would believe it more than if it showed up at the school parking lot in the morning."

Abner hesitates. "This is kind of a lot to ask."

Katarina flies over and yanks on his ear as hard as she can.

Which is pretty hard.

Then she yells into it, "A fairy godmother changed your life! Now a fairy godmother needs your help! Give Martin Shembly a break!"

"And besides . . ." I say, "wouldn't it be really cool to see your little pickle carnival full-size?"

He looks at me, thinking. Suddenly, he breaks into a smile, and even though he's old, I think I can see what he looked like when he was a happy little kid on Christmas morning. "It wouldn't just be cool—it would be really, really, *really* cool!"

"So you'll do it?" I ask.

"Yes! And I want to be the very first one to ride on the Terrifica roller coaster."

Yay! He'll do it! Before he has a chance to change his mind, I say, "I'll be back first thing in the morning with Martin and my friends Paige and Sunny." Then I think of something. "How are we going to get here? It's too far to hike, and I'm really bad with pumpkins."

"I'll take care of it," Abner says. Then he asks Katarina, "How *is* Terrifica?"

"She retired to Disney World in Florida. Next time you're on 'It's a Small World,' say hello."

He says, "She lives on the ride? Doesn't that song drive her crazy?"

"There's a rumor that she *wrote* that song," Katarina says.

Splurch! Splurch! Splurch!

Katarina and I roll our way back home surrounded by seeds and goo again. But we're not in a pumpkin; we're in a cantaloupe. (It's the only thing Abner had in his kitchen.)

And it's *still* a stupid way to travel.

CHAPTER
36

Right after dawn, there's a knock on my front door. When Mom and Dad answer it, they're very surprised to see Abner on the porch and his long green limousine parked in the driveway.

"Hello there," he says. "Lacey's probably told you I'm sponsoring a replacement carnival at my lake house today. I need to borrow your daughter and her friends to help set things up."

This is the first, scary test of whether our "Abner's Pickles Carnival" story is going to work. And—it does! Mom and Dad are thrilled that Abner is going to help the school.

And the story works with Dr. Harrington, and Sunny's mom, too. So that's why Sunny, Paige, Katarina, and I are now riding in the green limo nervously playing with the automatic windows while Abner is up front driving.

Paige asks Katarina, "Don't you need to be in Lacey's room watching the portal?"

Katarina shakes her head, "The portal was frozen solid this morning. Nothing's getting through without an ice pick."

Sunny presses a button that makes the glass between us and the limo's front seat slide down. "Mr. Abner, why are you doing the driving yourself?"

"All this would have been a little hard to explain to my driver, don't you think? I gave my entire staff the weekend off."

"*Smart*," Sunny says.

We park a block from Martin's house, and I climb out and walk the rest of the way. I get there just in time to see a car pulling out of Martin's driveway. His parents are in the front of the car and Martin's in the back. *I'm too late!* They're going to his violin audition! How am I going to stop them?

I consider throwing a rock at the car (I know that's a stupid idea, but it's the only one I have). Then I remember I've got a magic wand. But what spell should I use? Right before the car turns the corner—and gets out of range of my wand—I chant, "Hubble bubble, engine trouble!"

As soon as I toss the spell, the engine makes a wheezing, coughing, clunking sound and the car lurches to a stop.

I hide behind a neighbor's fence as Martin and his parents get out of the car. His father starts to open the hood, but his mother says, "We don't have time for that! We'll take my car."

They hurry back to the driveway, where a second car is parked. I raise my wand again and chant, "Double bubble, engine trouble!" I toss the spell just as Martin's father gets in and turns the key. The coughs, wheezes, and clunks are even louder this time. The car doesn't budge an inch, but a couple of pink bubbles float out from its radiator grille and drift through the yard.

Martin, who's waiting on the sidewalk with his mom, sees the bubbles and looks around suspiciously. I wiggle my fingers at him from behind the fence, and he smiles.

Unless Martin's parents have another car stashed away, I've solved the problem: Martin is not going to his audition.

Martin's mom pulls out her cell phone, exasperated. "Oh, for the love of Christmas! I'm calling a cab."

Oh, for the love of Christmas is right! I'm going to be sitting behind this fence all morning!

Fifteen minutes later, a yellow cab pulls into the driveway. But I'm ready for it. I raise my wand and chant, "Triple bubble, engine trouble!"

I toss the spell, and the loudest coughing, wheezing, clunking sounds so far come out of the cab's engine. And this time, there's something extra. The cab's hood pops open, and pink bubbles pour out. I wasn't expecting this—I just stuck the word *bubble* into the spell because it rhymed with *trouble*. But words in spells count, and when the word is bubbles—especially triple bubbles—you get a lot of them. I feel a little sorry for the cabdriver, whose engine won't work until midnight. On the bright side, his car is going to be really, really clean.

Martin's mother, whose mouth is a thin, angry line, says, "This is ridiculous! I'm calling another cab!" But as she pulls out her cell phone, Martin's father stops her. "Pamela, it's no use. We're not going to make it to the audition in time."

"But—"

"These things happen. We'll try to reschedule for next week." Then he puts his hand on Martin's shoulder. "I'm sorry, son. I know how disappointed you must be."

Martin plasters on a sad face and says, "Oh, I'm *horribly* disappointed."

Martin's mother punches another number into her cell phone. What if, after all this, she's still not ready to give up and she's going to rent a bus or a small airplane or something? She talks into the phone, "Hello, Maestro Chaliapin? I'm so sorry. Something unexpected has come up and we'll need to reschedule."

Yay! I don't have to bubble-ize a bus or an airplane! I pop out from behind the fence and act like I'm just noticing Martin in the driveway. "Hi, Martin! Have you heard the big news? Abner's Pickles is sponsoring a new school carnival today! Want to come?"

Martin looks at his father with big, puppy-dog eyes. "Can I, Dad? Can I?"

His father nods. "I don't see why not."

Double, triple, and quadruple yay!

On the way to Abner's house, I ask him to stop at the deserted school parking lot. The sun is shining bright and clear—which makes the remains of yesterday's carnival look really, really awful. With all the wet, limp cardboard, it looks like somebody tried to papier-mâché the pavement. Somebody who flunked art class.

The saddest thing of all is the pile of soggy stuffed animals that were supposed to be prizes. Yesterday they were soft and fluffy; now they're garbage. But I *need* them! It's one thing to feed people magic food; it will just disappear from their stomachs at midnight. But it's mean to give them magic prizes that won't be there in the morning.

So I get out of the limo, raise my wand, and chant, "Poor little animals wet and dirty, dry off and clean up in a hurry." I toss it at the animals, and they rise into the air, spin around, and then land in a perfect, clean, fuzzy pyramid.

We load them into the limo. And now it's finally carnival time.

CHAPTER 37

I carry Abner's miniature carnival out of the house and put it at the edge of the wide, green lawn. It's still so early that birds are hunting for worms in the morning dew—they don't know that they're about to see some serious magic.

There's quite a group out here on the grass: me, Katarina, Martin, Sunny, Paige, and Abner. My hands are a little sweaty—what if I mess this up? The carnival is pretty much our last chance.

"Take a deep breath and relax, Lacey," Katarina says. "Don't think about the many, many times you've bungled, botched, and butchered even the simplest of spells."

"KATARINA!" I shout.

"That's what I get for trying to be supportive," Katarina says.

I *do* take a deep breath, raise my wand, and chant, "Little carnival so tiny, turn big, bold, and shiny!"

I toss the spell at the carnival toy. Flashes of green, sparkly light shoot out from it like fireworks as the startled birds on the lawn flutter away and perch in the trees.

The fireworks go up, up, and up, and then crash back to the ground with a burst of sparkles.

With every sparkle burst, a booth or a sign or a ride appears.

Flash! There's a merry-go-round.

Flash! There's a teacup ride.

Flash! Flash! Flash! There's a drop tower, a super slide with five tracks, a Tilt-a-Whirl, the Terrifica roller coaster, and a gigantic Ferris wheel. And just like in the carnival toy, pickles decorate *everything*. The merry-go-round doesn't have horses to ride, it has pickles; the Ferris wheel has pickle-shaped gondolas; and the teacups aren't really teacups, they're pickle jars.

Flash-flash-flash! Food booths spring into view like pages in a pop-up book, all of them selling something either pickle-y or green or both. Pickles on sticks. Green cotton candy. Neon-bright jugs of green soda. Tubs of green relish for the hamburgers and hot dogs. Green ice cream. (I sure hope it's not pickle fla-vored.) Apple-green snow cones.

Flash-flash-flash! And we've got the carnival games: Whac-A-Pickle, pickle toss, tic-tac-pickle.

And, finally, the fuzzy animals float out of the open door of the limousine and over to the booths to be the prizes.

So less than a minute after I toss the spell, we have a

complete, full-sized, pickle-themed carnival, all set up and ready to go. I tell the others, "Now all we need to do is turn on the lights and the music! Instant carnival!"

"Are we going to do everything ourselves?" Martin asks. "Sell the tickets, run the rides, cook the food . . ."

". . . and cheat the rubes at the carnie games?" Katarina asks, a little hopefully.

"We're not cheating anybody!" I say. "But we *are* going to need some help." I look at the carnival, where the curious birds are flying back out of the trees and perching on the booths, hoping for food.

I raise my wand and chant, "On the count of three, workers you shall be! One, two three!" I toss the spell at the birds, which, with the sound of flapping wings, transform into carnival workers who wear pickle-green T-shirts. The newly human workers huddle together, heads bobbing, and give me one-eyed bird stares. (Which makes sense, since they were birds just a second ago.)

I tell them, "Everybody spread out! Choose a booth or a ride!" But they all just turn their heads to stare at me with their *other* eyes.

"Shoo!" I say, clapping my hands. "Get to work!"

They scramble off and the carnival comes to life. Lights are turned on. The merry-go-round spins with its organ playing. Delicious smells waft over from the food booths.

Katarina says, "Ooh, pretty!" and starts to fly toward the glittering lights. She never can resist anything that sparkles.

I jump in front of her to block her view. "Katarina! Snap out of it!"

Katarina blinks at me, a little dazed. "You need to warn me before you turn on twinkle lights!" She pulls a pair of dark glasses out of her pocket and puts them on. Superman has Kryptonite; Katarina has glitter.

I raise my arms dramatically and say, "Ladies and gentlemen! Welcome to the Lincoln Middle School Carnival!"

Martin says, "Small problem: there *are* no ladies and gentlemen."

Abner scratches his cowboy hat and tells me, "We're ten miles from town. How do you expect anyone to find out about us?"

Everyone looks at me like they think I've got the answer.

But I don't. I've been so busy planning a carnival that I never thought about the people.

Paige sees my blank look. "Oh, no! We've gone to all this trouble so Makayla won't think it's a magic carnival . . . and now it's not going to matter, because no one's going to know about it!"

O.

M.

G.

I start jumping up and down excitedly.

Katarina gives me a cranky look. "What's wrong with you, Lacey? Do you have fleas?"

"No! I have an idea," I say. "We need Makayla. And we need her *now*."

They all look at me like I'm insane. But I'm not insane. I'm a *genius*.

Thirty-four minutes later, Makayla stands in front of the pickle carnival talking breathlessly into Taylor's camera. "This is Makayla Brandice, your eyes and ears on the school—with an exclusive, worldwide breaking news report! I'm here at the fabulous vacation compound of Abner, of Abner's Pickles fame. And, today only, he's putting on a fund-raising carnival to benefit Lincoln Middle School!"

She rushes up to Abner, who stands near the entrance to the Terrifica roller coaster with Martin. "Mr. Abner! Please tell us where you got this wonderful idea!"

Abner puts his arm around Martin's shoulders and says, "It wasn't my idea. Your classmate Martin Shembly talked me into it. He's a wonderful kid, and you all are very lucky to have him at your school."

Makayla nods. "Oh, that's what I've always said, Mr. Abner! We're so very, very lucky to have Martin."

Makayla is *shameless*! But at least this time she's shameless

on the side of good. She turns back to the camera. "So, whatever you do, come to the carnival! It's amazing! I'm spreading the word, and I want you to spread the word, too! Tweet it! Text it! Call everybody you know! Let's make this the most successful fund-raiser in Lincoln's history! We'll repair the water tower. And I'll get to go to the Online News Association banquet."

That's a little extra shameless, even for her. So she adds, "It's not about me, of course. It's about the school! Please come!"

Because of Makayla, thirty-eight minutes later, the word is out.

But will people come?

CHAPTER 38

Yes, they do!

Thanks to Makayla's gigantic mouth and pushy personality (which, as of now, I *love*), by ten a.m., hundreds of people have bought tickets. The morning goes by in a pickle-green blur. Tons of people shake Martin's hand, including Principal Conehurst, whose smile is so wide that it stretches almost all the way around his head.

While Martin greets the public, Sunny, Paige, and I work at the pickle-shaped ticket booth. Katarina leans against a pile of money, out of sight. She says, "Cash is surprisingly comfortable!"

As more and more people arrive, there are long lines for everything, but no one seems to mind. This is a pretty small town, and there hasn't been a carnival this good in . . . *ever*, probably.

The kid who seems to like the carnival best isn't a kid at all—it's Abner. He rides all the pickle rides, plays all the games, and eats all the food. Every time he sees me, he says, "This is the best day of my life!"

After lunch, Mom, Dad, and Madison come up to the ticket window, all smiles.

"The carnival's wonderful, Lacey!" Dad tells me through the little window.

"Congratulations, honey!" Mom says. "It's just amazing that Abner's Pickles came through like this."

Madison pulls on Mom's and Dad's sleeves. "Come on! I want a pickle snow cone! I want to ride the teacups! I want to play Whac-A-Pickle!"

Dad smiles at her. "Is that all?"

"No. I want you to win me seven stuffed animals! So I can sleep with a different one every night."

Dad hands me all the cash in his wallet. "This is going to be an expensive afternoon."

I hand Dad the tickets, and Madison yanks them away.

Mom calls, "We're only here for an hour—then it's back to the Hungry Moose for the dinner shift. Good luck today, Lacey!"

"Thanks, Mom."

As the day goes on, I'm excited to see the pile of cash below the ticket booth windows getting bigger and bigger. Katarina puts on a little green visor and snaps pink rubber bands around bundles of cash and then stacks them in the back of the booth.

Sunny, Paige, and I take turns either selling tickets or walking around the carnival. Every time I leave the booth, I'm happy to see that the bird-workers are doing surprisingly well. They're manning (birding?) the rides just fine. And this has got to be the cleanest carnival ever. The second anybody drops a piece of popcorn or any other food, they scramble for it and pop it into their mouths. Weird and gross, but very tidy.

The afternoon shadows are getting long as I finish another shift in the ticket booth and head out into the carnival again. I see a familiar face at the snow cone stand.

"Hi, Scott!"

"Hi, Lacey," he says as he walks past me. Wow! He's not even going to stop! Even with all that's going on, I can't leave things like this. So I blurt out, "Scott? Are you mad at me?"

This makes him stop.

"No, I'm not mad," he says.

"You never really talk to me anymore."

"You're always busy with Martin. You haven't even come to a Uni-Cyclones meeting."

Oh, geez. I can't tell Scott I'm busy with Martin because I'm his fairy godmother—but what *do* I tell Scott? Finally, I say, "After the water tower thing, Martin needed my help—you saw how bad it was for him. But when the carnival is over, he won't need my help anymore and I'll have more time for things like the Uni-Cyclones."

He's quiet for a long time, and I think I've blown it. But then he says, "The next meeting is on Monday."

"I'll be there!"

He smiles a little, more with his eyes—and those beautiful eyelashes of his—than with his mouth. "Great," he says.

Then I gulp and ask a question that's a lot scarier than the pickle Tilt-a-Whirl. "Scott? Do you want to ride the Ferris wheel with me?"

"Yeah," Scott says. "I'd like that."

CHAPTER

39

The sun is setting as Scott and I climb into the pickle-shaped gondola of the Ferris wheel. A sleepy-eyed bird-worker closes the safety bar over our laps and turns a key on the control panel to put the wheel in motion.

I always forget how high up Ferris wheels go. You're in a tiny car that you could fall out of at any second—and you're going up and up and up. When the gondola rocks a little, I grab the safety bar.

Scott sees my white knuckles and gives me a smile. "It is pretty high, isn't it?"

He puts his hand over mine.

He *likes* me.

At least I think he likes me. But maybe he's just worried about me freaking out on the Ferris wheel and embarrassing him in front of the whole school.

I let go of the safety bar, to show him I'm not afraid. But as the Ferris wheel turns around and around in the last rays of the sun, Scott keeps holding my hand.

He likes me!

The Ferris wheel slows to a stop to unload people at the bottom, and our car sways at the very top. It's like we're floating up here, peaceful and alone.

Scott's really nice—and he *likes* me. And all I really seem to do is lie to him. Maybe it's time for the truth. "Scott, I want to tell you something," I say.

He looks at me, curious.

"I . . . I'm . . ."

But just before I say, *I'm a fairy godmother, with a magic wand and everything, and I hope you still like me even though it's kind of strange,* there are shouts down on the ground.

"STOP THE RIDE!"

We both peer down at the ground, far below us. There are more shouts: "Get us off this thing!" "I'm gonna be *sick!*" "Please help us!"

"What's happening?" Scott asks.

And then I notice that there are no bird-workers at the controls for the rides. Not one! They can't have just disappeared—it's not midnight yet!

But they're definitely gone. And all the rides are still spinning and twirling and looping and dropping. No wonder everybody's yelling.

Scott and I are actually the lucky ones. We're just stuck—forty feet above the ground with no way to get off!

Down at the ride control stations, people in the crowd are trying to turn things off by pushing every button they can find. Nothing helps.

"Why can't they shut the rides down?" Scott asks.

"I think you need a key for them."

What am I going to do? I can't use my magic wand in front of Scott, Makayla, and all these people, but I've got to do *something*. I start working out a plan in my head:

Step one: put Scott to sleep so he won't see me doing any magic. (Where's the Good Night Moonstone when I need it?)

Step two: make myself invisible so I can fly down to the ground.

Step three: come up with a good flying spell. (Now I really wish I'd paid more attention in magic homeschooling.)

Step four: zap up a magic key I can use to turn the rides off.

Geez. This is complicated.

Step five: start over and come up with a better plan.

Scott says, "Look at that guy down there!"

Down at the control station for the Tilt-a-Whirl, there's a small figure who's opening the front panel and pulling out wires. It's a boy with glasses and dark-brown hair. And not just any boy—it's *Martin*!

I have a horrible, sinking feeling. Martin's track record has been pretty shaky so far. What if he does something that makes the Tilt-a-Whirl whirl off into space? It could happen—after all, he wrecked a whole water tower!

I shriek and cover my eyes when sparks fly out of the control panel that Martin's working on. I wait for the screams and the crash.

"He did it!" Scott says.

Peering out between my fingers, I look down and see the Tilt-a-Whirl coming to stop. The riders get off it, so dizzy that they walk in loopy circles until they finally just sit down on the ground. But they're all safe.

The loudest screams come from the Terrifica roller coaster, where a dozen people ride the train of cars up and down the scary-high tracks, faster and faster. I squint—Abner's in the very front car. I bet right about now he's really wishing he hadn't had five servings of green cotton candy today.

Martin runs over to the Terrifica's control station and yanks it open. As he fiddles with the wires, it's like one of those scary scenes in movies where a guy's trying to stop the timer for a bomb. In the movies, it's always the red wire. Or is it the blue wire? Oh, please, Martin! Get it right!

To my relief, there's one last burst of sparks from the control station, and the roller coaster cars glide down to the platform, smooth as anything. Abner gives Martin a grateful look—and then barfs into his cowboy hat. Yay and ew.

It takes Martin only a few more minutes to shut down all of the runaway rides, and now the merry-go-round, the drop tower, and the teacups all slow to a stop. Martin gets a lot of pats on the back and at least seven kisses.

The Ferris wheel comes last, which is only fair since we're not moving. Martin hot-wires the controls and gets people off, one car at time. He gets a lot more pats and kisses—he's a hero!

As we wait our turn, Scott says, "You were going to tell me something. What was it?"

There's been enough excitement for one night, so I just say, "Uh . . . um . . . do you want to go to a movie sometime?"

There's a long, long silence. Then he smiles and says, "Sure. That would be fun."

I know what you're thinking. *No, he's not my boyfriend.*

But ask me again in a month.

After the last people get off the Ferris wheel, the kids cluster around Martin, applauding and cheering while he grins. I'm pretty sure Martin has never, ever gotten this kind of attention. But he sure deserves it.

The kids may all be happy and excited, but the grown-ups look terrified.

Principal Conehurst shouts, "Is anybody hurt?" He scans the

crowd, and when no one says anything, he gives a sigh of relief.

And Abner pushes his way to the front, blotting his forehead with a handkerchief. "All right, folks! We've had a lot of fun, but now it's time to call it a day."

Oh, no! The carnival was supposed to go on for hours more—and we need to raise all the money we can get. We've *got* to start it back up!

But then I look around at all the sparking wires and empty booths, and I know we can't. *Agh!* Antarctica, here I come. Martin may be a hero right now, but tomorrow the kids will remember about the water tower and the field trips and his life will still stink. And so will mine!

Suddenly, there are cries of "Help! Help!"

My heart skips a beat. Maybe people *are* hurt.

The yells are coming from the ticket booth. "HELP! HELP!" Inside, Paige and Sunny are pressed against the ticket window. The bundles of money—and there are a lot of them—have fallen all around them.

Sunny presses her mouth against the slot in the window. "We can't get out! The money fell over!"

I run around to the ticket booth's back door and turn the handle. The door opens, and pink-rubber-banded cash pours out like a Las Vegas slot machine paying off.

Paying off *big*.

Makayla starts shrieking. "LOOK AT ALL THAT MONEY! LOOK AT ALL THAT MONEY!"

Martin and Principal Conchurst reach the booth at the same time and watch as Sunny and Paige crawl out through all the cash. I've never seen that much money in one place.

The principal turns to Martin and says, "We'll have to count it, of course, but to me it looks like there's more than enough money here to fix the water tower, restore the field trips, and . . ."

He gets a gleam in his eye.

". . . buy that espresso machine for the teachers' lounge."

Makayla shrieks and kisses Martin right on the lips.

(Ew.)

I peer into the booth, and I see Katarina peeking out from behind a stack of cash. She smiles and gives me a thumbs-up.

I hug Martin. "I think your life officially doesn't stink anymore."

CHAPTER 40

Right before midnight, Abner, Martin, Sunny, Paige, Katarina, and I sit on deck chairs on Abner's patio waiting to see the magic carnival disappear.

Oh—and we found the bird-workers. They all climbed up into trees, where they're sleeping with their heads tucked under their arms. (If you ever use magic bird-workers, remember they're only good till dusk. After that, they want to go home to roost.)

The birds aren't the only ones who are asleep—so is Abner. He had a really big, fun day at the carnival, and the second he sat down in his chair, he conked out like Madison after a birthday party.

I'm sorry to say that it took quite a bit of lying for us kids to be here right now. Paige's father is working the late shift at the hospital, so Paige told him she had a sleepover at my house. Sunny and I told our parents that we had a sleepover at Paige's house. And Martin told his parents that he was helping late on the carnival cleanup crew, which would look very good on his college applications.

Martin checks his watch. "A minute till midnight! That's *synnngera* in Elvish."

Katarina snorts. "That means 'I have dandruff.' Where do you get these words? I'm serious. Where?"

Martin blushes. "Off the Internet. Maybe I should have learned Troll instead."

Katarina nods encouragingly. "Troll is easy! Instead of talking, they hit each other on the head with clubs. Excellent language, but very painful."

Paige laughs and tells Martin, "Maybe you should try Spanish."

As the seconds count down, Sunny tells me, "You're getting better at being a fairy godmother, Lacey. Usually you're running around like crazy about now. But tonight you're done early!"

"I admit things are looking positive," Katarina says. "But remember, the moon isn't officially full until 12:34 a.m. A lot can happen in half an hour."

I shake my head. "Nothing's going to happen! I've finished my fairy godmother assignment. We raised a lot of money, and the kids like Martin, so his life doesn't stink anymore. Makayla even kissed him! We've done it."

"And I got out of my violin audition. It was a perfect day!"

The bells of the town's clock start chiming midnight, and Abner wakes up with a start.

"Did I miss anything?" he says sleepily.

"You're just in time," I say.

Green fireworks shoot out of all the rides and booths, which disappear one by one. Then the fireworks join together in one brilliant blast overhead. A moment later, *PLUNK!* Abner's miniature carnival toy falls back to the lawn.

And, finally, the bird-workers in the trees sparkle back into real birds again. There's a lot of confused chirping and cheeping.

I look around at the empty lawn, which, with the minutes-from-being-full moon overhead, is almost as bright as day. Sunny's right. I *am* getting better at this.

Suddenly, a purple jewel lights up on Katarina's dress and she looks at it, horrified. "This can't be happening!" she says.

"What's wrong?" I ask.

The purple jewel starts to play a tune that sounds familiar.

Martin cocks his head. "What song is that?"

Paige says, "Don't ask me. I'm tone deaf."

Sunny listens for a second. "It's from the 'It's a Small World' ride at Disney World."

Katarina shrieks, *"And it means Terrifica is on her way!* Everybody hide!"

Too late—a tiny, glowing dot of purple light zigzags toward us and flies onto the patio. It turns out to be a very, very, old fairy godmother with dark-purple hair, a wrinkled face, and enormous ears that could belong to a bat. And she looks *furious*. "What are you idiots doing here?" she shouts.

Katarina gulps. "What do you mean?"

Terrifica pokes Katarina with her wand, exactly the same way Katarina pokes me. "I am the best fairy godmother teacher who has ever taught," she shouts. "Not one of my students has been a failure! There are no dryer fairies or dung beetle fairies among my alumnae! And now you, Katarina, are about to be banished to Antarctica."

"But—" Katarina says.

"SILENCE!" Terrifica shouts. "Katarina, they never should have let you into the Godmother Academy. Of all my students, you were always the most trouble! Always getting your spells wrong. Never finishing your book reports. Always talking back in class."

Gee. Katarina kind of sounds like me.

Forget kind of. She *really* sounds like me.

I expect Katarina to start shouting back, but she just hangs her head miserably. A tear trickles down her cheek.

Now it's my turn to get mad. Katarina is a cranky pain sometimes, but she doesn't deserve this. After all, she did agree to homeschool me when it would have been a lot easier for her to just let me get shipped off to the Godmother Academy.

"She's *not* a failure," I say.

"SILENCE!"

"I won't be silent! Katarina's a great teacher. And we're not going to Antarctica! We got Martin his dream."

"No, you didn't, you dunderhead! Why do you think I flew all the way here from Florida during the international mah-jongg tournament? To stop you and Katarina from ruining my perfect reputation, that's why!"

"What are you talking about?" I ask.

Terrifica glares at me and points into the distance with her wand. We all look and see a single, puffy white cloud far in the distance. "That cloud is directly over your house, Lacey. It's a blizzard straight from the South Pole, waiting to blow you and Katarina away at twelve thirty-four a.m."

"That can't be right," I say. "I did everything! I totally unstinked Martin's life!"

Terrifica shakes her head. "No, you didn't."

"What haven't I done?"

"I can't tell you that. It's between you and your client."

The fairy godmothers always, always, *always* make this stuff so hard! I turn to Martin and peer into his face. "Martin! What's wrong with your life? Why is it still stinking?"

Martin says, "Um . . . well . . . everything's fine."

I yank his shirt. "No it's not! Tell me what's wrong! I'm your fairy godmother and I need to know!"

"Lacey, you're kind of creeping me out here."

Katarina flies up to us. "Tell her! We only have twenty-two minutes before the moon is full!"

Martin looks totally blank.

"This is important!" I shout. "What is still wrong with your life?"

Paige pats me on the shoulder, "Lacey. He's a boy. Boys don't talk about feelings."

Sunny says, "He did with me, sometimes."

I let go of Martin's shirt. Then I yank Sunny's shirt. (I'm doing a lot of yanking tonight, but it's an emergency.) "Sunny! What did he tell you? What else about Martin's life needs to be fixed? Think! Think! Think!"

CHAPTER 41

"To Martin's in a flash, and don't let us crash!" I chant. A split second later, we skid onto the lawn in front of his house, stopping so fast that our feet dig deep grooves in the grass.

"That was cool!" Martin says.

"That was *scary*," I say as we race through the front door of Martin's house. The clock in the hallway shows 12:29 a.m.

Martin calls up the staircase that leads to the second floor, "Mom! Dad! I need to talk to you! MOM! DAD!"

A few moments later, Martin's parents rush out of their bedroom, pulling on bathrobes.

"What's wrong?" his dad asks.

Martin rushes up the stairs and stands next to them, looking very short and defenseless. "I need to tell you guys something. Something very important."

"What is it, Martin?" his mother says.

He gulps. "Ah . . . well . . . I . . ."

Our time's almost gone! If we weren't on such a tight deadline, I'd let Martin get to this his way. But we've only got five minutes. By now, probably just four minutes!

So I rush up the stairs and jump in, mouth first. "Martin's life stinks."

They look at me, shocked.

But I keep going; there's nothing else I can do. "I know you think Martin's a musical genius, and maybe he is. And I know that you're excited about getting him lessons with that maestro guy. But Martin doesn't want to do it."

Now they look at Martin, shocked.

"But you *love* the violin," his mother says.

Martin still doesn't seem ready to take a stand.

"He doesn't love the violin," I say. "He likes the violin, and he's good at it, and he'll always play it. But what he loves is inventing things. Sure, everything he makes blows up or farts or knocks something down. But that's because he spends all his time practicing the violin when he doesn't want to!"

Martin frowns. "Not *everything* I make blows up or farts!"

"Martin! We don't have time for this!" I turn back to his parents. "You guys have got to let Martin be Martin and forget about the musical genius part—or his life is going to stink forever!"

Martin's mom looks worried. "Martin, you don't really think your life stinks, do you?"

This sounds funny coming from Martin's very-proper mother, but it's the most important question she'll ever ask.

Two minutes before the full moon! I want to jump in here, but I think Martin is going to have to answer this question on his own. He looks at both his parents as if he's terrified to tell them the truth. But finally, he says, "Kinda."

"Kinda?" his father asks.

Martin nods. "Yes, it stinks! I hate all the practicing! But you guys only seem to like me when I'm playing!"

Wow. Especially for a boy, that's an amazing thing to say out loud. How will his parents take it?

As the seconds keep ticking away, they seem frozen in place. Finally, after what seems like forever, Martin's father puts his arms around him and hugs him. "I love you *all* the time," his father says.

And then, to my ginormous relief, Martin's mother hugs him, too. "What are you thinking? Of course I love you all the time."

Martin looks up and studies their faces. "You'd love me even if I never played the violin again?"

They both nod without hesitating a moment.

"So . . . I don't have to take lessons with Maestro Chaliapin?" he asks.

His parents both shake their heads. "No, you don't," his father says.

Martin hugs them back.

Then Martin's father looks over at me. "By the way . . . who *are* you?"

"I'm just a friend," I say.

"She's more than a friend," Martin says. "She's my *maar* friend."

Martin's father asks, "You mean she's your great and excellent friend?"

"Dad! You speak Elvish?"

"I'm a lot more like you than you think," his father says, giving Martin another hug.

Martin smiles. "I hear my accent is awful."

"That's all right, honey!" his mother says. "We'll get you a *tutor*!"

At 12:42 a.m., I leave the house and see Abner's green limo waiting for me at the curb. I climb in and find Abner at the wheel with Terrifica sitting on his shoulder. Sunny and Paige are in the back.

Sunny asks, "Did you fix things?"

"I think so. But with fairy godmother stuff, it's so hard to tell. Where's Katarina?"

Paige says, "She flew to your house to see if the blizzard is still there."

Sunny whispers in my ear, "I don't think she wanted to be in the same car as Terrifica."

Terrifica's bat ears quiver. "I heard that!"

About a block away from my house, Terrifica yells, *"STOP! It's Katarina!"* Abner slams on the brakes.

Katarina flies up to my window, looking grim and shaking her head. "It's awful! Just awful!"

OMG! After all this, it didn't work.

There's silence in the car as Abner drives the final block. I expect the worst: a giant glacier, maybe.

But there's no glacier.

No snow or icicles.

No mysterious cloud overhead.

Just my house, looking cozy and normal in the moonlight. Even the weeds in the front yard are still there.

I look at Katarina. "You said it was awful!"

"It *is*! The paint is peeling. The lawn is a disgrace. And there are cracks in the sidewalk."

"But there's no snow!"

"Snow would cover up a multitude of sins. I can't believe that this is where I'm going to be living for the foreseeable future."

I'm on the verge of yelling at her for badmouthing my beautiful house, and then it sinks in: if Katarina's going to be living here for the foreseeable future, we're not going to Antarctica! *We're not going anyplace!*

"We did it!" I shout.

Everyone in the car cheers. Even Terrifica, who says, "Thank glitter! My record is *perfect.*"

CHAPTER 42

The next morning, Katarina sits on the edge of my dresser, looking glum even though the temperature is back to normal and there's not a penguin in sight.

"Room sweet room," she says, sounding sarcastic about it. Instead of complaining about my room, you'd think she'd be happy not to be in Antarctica right now.

"*I* like it this way." I flop down on the bed. "You can change your sixty percent into anything you want."

"Why bother? No matter what I do, it's never quite right. Underneath, it's still your room, not mine." She climbs into my jewelry box and pulls the lid shut over her.

I feel bad. After all this time, she still doesn't feel at home here. But what can I do about it?

There's a glittery blue flash at the window: it's Augustina Oberon. Just what I need. *Another* fairy. I look at the jewelry box—Katarina peers out for a second and then quietly closes the lid again. Great! So I'm the one who has to talk to her.

"Hello, Augustina," I say.

"So, Lacey Unger-Ware, it seems you completed your assignment with twelve seconds to spare last night. Cutting it a little close, weren't you?"

"But I got it done!"

"I've brought your report card."

"I get graded?"

"Of course. With every assignment."

Augustina snaps her fingers, and a sheet of sparkly paper floats down from the ceiling.

I read it and frown. "I got a C-minus?"

"You were lucky to get that! I wanted to give you a D, but Terrifica said that anybody who could put up with Katarina deserves a little extra credit, and I was forced to agree."

And with a flash of blue, she disappears.

A moment later, Katarina pokes her head back out of the jewelry box. "Is she gone?" she asks.

"Yes."

"She's lucky. *I'm* still stuck right here."

Geez. I've got to do something to cheer her up.

Compared to that, unstinking Martin's life was easy.

CHAPTER 43

Today, the whole school is gathered around the new Abraham Lincoln top hat water tower for the rededication ceremony. The tower looks exactly the same as it was before, except not rusty or filled with slimy, disgusting water. For today's event, there's a wide purple-and-gold ribbon tied around the legs.

Principal Conehurst finishes a long speech about how wonderful it is to have the water tower back, and everyone cheers. Then he says, "Martin Shembly will now cut the ribbon."

Mrs. Fleecy hands Martin a giant pair of gold scissors, and Martin slices through the ribbon in one smooth motion. We're all about to cheer again when we notice that the ribbon isn't quite cut through. Martin raises his hand. "I've got this covered."

He pulls on the ribbon, which still doesn't tear. Then he yanks really hard—and there's a loud cracking sound from the tower's legs. "Oops," Martin says.

"Run for your lives!" Principal Conehurst shouts. And the water tower tips over in a gigantic flood of icy cold water. Makayla, who's the closest, gets washed away screaming, "Not again!"

Kidding! I was just daydreaming.

Actually, the rededication ceremony went perfectly. The speeches were a little boring (and that's when I started daydreaming about Martin knocking over the water tower again), but Martin manages to cut the ribbon without a smidge of trouble.

"Thank you, Martin!" Principal Conehurst says. "The entire school owes you an enormous debt of gratitude for helping raise the money."

Martin says, "I couldn't have done it without a lot of help. Makayla Brandice, you're a publicity genius."

From behind her camera, Makayla waves at the crowd, and we exchange a smile. (And it's sooo weird that we don't hate each other anymore. Let's see how long *that* lasts.)

Martin continues, "And Sunny Varden, Paige Harrington, and especially Lacey Unger-Ware, you're all wonderful. Get up and take a bow!"

And we do.

After school, Mrs. Fleecy walks into the art room carrying two extra-large containers of crafts supplies and cookies. She smiles when she sees Martin sitting next to me, Sunny, and Paige. "Martin? Are you joining Craft-N-Crunch?"

He shakes his head. "No, I'm just here to help the girls with some wiring."

"How nice! They've been working so hard on their project."

Then Scott pokes his head in the door. "Come on, Martin! You need to start the Future Flyers Club meeting. The leaf blowers are here!"

"Where'd they come from, Martin?" I ask.

"Abner donated them! He says I remind him of himself when he was a kid." Martin looks a little worried. "Don't tell Principal Conehurst we're working on jetpacks."

I won't need to tell him—the principal's sure to notice when they knock something down. But, thank glitter, that's not my problem anymore. "Be sure to wear helmets! And knee pads! And maybe some Bubble Wrap!" I say.

As Martin gets up to go, Scott tells me, "See you tomorrow, Lacey."

"I can't wait," I say.

After the boys leave, Sunny asks me, "What's tomorrow?"

"Um . . . we're going to a movie."

Sunny and Paige both say, "Ooooh."

I pretend like it's no big deal, but on the inside, I'm saying, "Ooooh," too.

CHAPTER 44

I put a shoe box down on my dresser, where Katarina, looking bored, sits filing her nails.

"I made you something," I say. "Sunny, Paige, and Martin all helped."

She barely looks up from her nails. "Great. A shoe box. I'll check it out later. Now, if you'll excuse me, my cuticles won't wait."

"No, *look!*" I say.

She sighs and walks over to it.

"I decided you need a space of your own in here. Someplace nice."

"And you thought of a shoe box," she says. "Yippee." She somehow makes "Yippee" sound like "Yuck."

I turn the box around to the side where I've made a Katarina-sized door. I open it. "Go inside."

"I'm not going into a shoe box!"

"Please!"

She looks inside the door. *"Oh,"* she says, and disappears inside.

When I don't hear another sound for a while, I peer through the window. Katarina is walking around the little room that we've made for her over the last two weeks, sometimes in Craft-N-Crunch and sometimes in Martin's basement.

"Oh, I love the wallpaper!" she says.

"Paige saw it in a magazine, and we copied it."

"And there's a TV!"

"It's Sunny's old smartphone. She thought you would like it."

"And there's a crystal chandelier!"

"I made it out of a necklace. Martin wired it with little lights. Turn it on!"

She looks at me, worried. "It's not going to blow up, is it?"

"No. Only the first two blew up. This one is fine."

Katarina flips the switch, and the tiny crystal chandelier sparkles with light.

"Lovely," she says.

Katarina pats the bed. "It feels comfortable."

"It's filled with feathers. I told Madison I'd eat her broccoli for a month if she'd let me have one of her feather boas."

Katarina sits on the bed, studying every detail of the room.

"And I didn't use one speck of magic, so nothing will disappear at midnight," I say. "It will last as long as you want to stay. Which, I hope, is a long time."

Katarina says, "You did all this for me?"

I nod. "This is your home. I want you to be happy."

Katarina says, "This could work."

And then she gets up and slams the door in my face.

I think that means she likes it.

ACKNOWLEDGMENTS

The Spell Bind's glittering godparents include Emily Bergman, John Biondo, Teresa Blasberg, Helen Brauner, Becky Bristow, Josh Capps, Jennifer Cheng, Jennifer Collopy, Delmus Credle (who tirelessly listened to never-ending details about jetpacks and pickles), Breezie Daniel, Dirk Dickens, Mike Hale, Russ Hanford, Michelle Hardy, Lisa Holmes, Alice Lawson, Laurie Mattson, Maelena Mattson, Jen Mulder, Jean Noble, Catherine Onder, Gerardo Paron, Daryl Patton, Michael Schenkman, Cheryl Tan, Linda Wachter, Daniel Wake, Alexis Wallrich, Justeen Ward, Marty Ward, and everyone at Once Upon a Time Bookstore in Montrose.

Laura Hopper, Joseph Veltre, and Bayard Maybank are our Godmother Posse. Thanks, guys!

Tracey Keevan, our wonderful editor, makes sure our spells never backfire unless we want them to.

And thanks with sparkles on top to Jamie Baker, our publicist, and the great team at Disney-Hyperion.